D1523471

FIRE!!

A Quarterly Devoted to the Younger Negro Artists

Premier Issue Edited by
WALLACE THURMAN

In Association With

Langston Hughes   Zora Neale Hurston
Gwendolyn Bennett   Aaron Douglas
Richard Bruce   John Davis

Table of Contents

Volume One   Number One

Martino Fine Books

Eastford, CT
2022

Martino Fine Books
P.O. Box 913,
Eastford, CT 06242 USA

ISBN 978-1-68422-660-3

Copyright 2022

Martino Fine Books

Cover Design Tiziana Matarazzo

Printed in the United States of America On 100% Acid-Free Paper

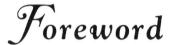

Foreword

FIRE . . . *flaming, burning, searing, and penetrating far beneath the superficial items of the flesh to boil the sluggish blood.*

FIRE . . . *a cry of conquest in the night, warning those who sleep and revitalizing those who linger in the quiet places dozing.*

FIRE . . . *melting steel and iron bars, poking livid tongues between stone apertures and burning wooden opposition with a cackling chuckle of contempt.*

FIRE . . . *weaving vivid, hot designs upon an ebon bordered loom and satisfying pagan thirst for beauty unadorned . . . the flesh is sweet and real . . . the soul an inward flush of fire. . . . Beauty? . . . flesh on fire—on fire in the furnace of life blazing. . . .*

> *"Fy-ah,*
> *Fy-ah, Lawd,*
> *Fy-ah gonna burn ma soul!"*

FIRE!
A Quarterly Devoted to the Younger Negro Artists

Wishes to Thank the Following Persons
Who Acted as Patrons
For the First Issue

MAURINE BOIE, *Minneapolis, Minn.*
NELLIE R. BRIGHT, *Philadelphia, Pa.*
ARTHUR HUFF FAUSET, *Philadelphia, Pa.*
DOROTHY HUNT HARRIS, *New York City*
ARTHUR P. MOOR, *Harrisburg, Pa.*
DOROTHY R. PETERSON, *Brooklyn, N. Y.*
MR. AND MRS. JOHN PETERSON, *New York City*
E. B. TAYLOR, *Baltimore, Md.*
CARL VAN VECHTEN, *New York City*

Being a non-commercial product interested only in the arts, it is necessary that we make some appeal for aid from interested friends. For the second issue of FIRE we would appreciate having fifty people subscribe ten dollars each, and fifty more to subscribe five dollars each.

We make no eloquent or rhetorical plea. FIRE speaks for itself.

Gratefully,
THE BOARD OF EDITORS.

FIRE!!

A Quarterly Devoted to the Younger Negro Artists

Premier Issue Edited by
WALLACE THURMAN

In Association With

Langston Hughes   Zora Neale Hurston
Gwendolyn Bennett   Aaron Douglas
Richard Bruce   John Davis

Table of Contents

Volume One   Number One

EDITORIAL OFFICES
314 West 138th Street, New York City

Price $1.00 per copy   Issued Quarterly

FIRE!!

DEVOTED TO YOUNGER NEGRO ARTISTS

Cordelia the Crude

Physically, if not mentally, Cordelia was a potential prostitute, meaning that although she had not yet realized the moral import of her wanton promiscuity nor become mercenary, she had, nevertheless, become quite blasé and bountiful in the matter of bestowing sexual favors upon persuasive and likely young men. Yet, despite her seeming lack of discrimination, Cordelia was quite particular about the type of male to whom she submitted, for numbers do not necessarily denote a lack of taste, and Cordelia had discovered after several months of active observation that one could find the qualities one admires or reacts positively to in a varied hodge-podge of outwardly different individuals.

The scene of Cordelia's activities was The Roosevelt Motion Picture Theatre on Seventh Avenue near 145th Street. Thrice weekly the program changed, and thrice weekly Cordelia would plunk down the necessary twenty-five cents evening admission fee, and saunter gaily into the foul-smelling depths of her favorite cinema shrine. The Roosevelt Theatre presented all of the latest pictures, also, twice weekly, treated its audiences to a vaudeville bill, then too, one could always have the most delightful physical contacts . . . hmm. . . .

Cordelia had not consciously chosen this locale nor had there been any conscious effort upon her part to take advantage of the extra opportunities afforded for physical pleasure. It had just happened that the Roosevelt Theatre was more close to her home than any other neighborhood picture palace, and it had also just happened that Cordelia had become almost immediately initiated into the ways of a Harlem theatre chippie soon after her discovery of the theatre itself.

It is the custom of certain men and boys who frequent these places to idle up and down the aisle until some female is seen sitting alone, to slouch down into a seat beside her, to touch her foot or else press her leg in such a way that it can be construed as accidental if necessary, and then, if the female is wise or else shows signs of willingness to become wise, to make more obvious approaches until, if successful, the approached female will soon be chatting with her baiter about the picture being shown, lolling in his arms, and helping to formulate plans for an after-theatre rendezvous. Cordelia had, you see, shown a willingness to become wise upon her second visit to The Roosevelt. In a short while she had even learned how to squelch the bloated, lewd faced Jews and eager middle aged Negroes who might approach as well as how to inveigle the likeable little yellow or brown half men, embryo avenue sweetbacks, with their well modeled heads, stickily plastered hair, flaming cravats, silken or broadcloth shirts, dirty underwear, low cut vests, form fitting coats, bell-bottom trousers and shiny shoes with metal cornered heels clicking with a brave, brazen rhythm upon the bare concrete floor as their owners angled and searched for prey.

Cordelia, sixteen years old, matronly mature, was an undisciplined, half literate product of rustic South Carolina, and had come to Harlem very much against her will with her parents and her six brothers and sisters. Against her will because she had not been at all anxious to leave the lackadaisical life of the little corn pone settlement where she had been born, to go trooping into the unknown vastness of New York, for she had been in love, passionately in love with one John Stokes who raised pigs, and who, like his father before him, found the raising of pigs so profitable that he could not even consider leaving Lintonville. Cordelia had blankly informed her parents that she would not go with them when they decided to be lured to New York by an older son who had remained there after the demobilization of the war time troops. She had even threatened to run away with John until they should be gone, but of course John could not leave his pigs, and John's mother was not very keen on having Cordelia for a daughter-in-law — those Joneses have bad mixed blood in 'em—so Cordelia had had to join the Gotham bound caravan and leave her lover to his succulent porkers.

However, the mere moving to Harlem had not doused the rebellious flame. Upon arriving Cordelia had not only refused to go to school and refused to hold even the most easily held job, but had also victoriously defied her harassed parents so frequently when it came to matters of discipline that she soon found herself with a mesmerizing lack of home restraint, for the stress of trying to maintain themselves and their family in the new environment was far too much of a task for Mr. and Mrs. Jones to attend to facilely and at the same time try to control a recalcitrant child. So, when Cordelia had refused either to work or to attend school, Mrs. Jones herself had gone out for day's work, leaving Cordelia at home to take care of their five room railroad flat, the front room of which was rented out to a couple "living together," and to see that the younger children, all of whom were of school age, made their four trips daily between home and the nearby public school—as well as see that they had their greasy, if slim, food rations and an occasional change of clothing. Thus Cordelia's days were full—and so were her nights. The only difference being that the days belonged to the folks at home while the nights (since the folks were too tired or too sleepy to know or care when she came in or went out) belonged to her and to—well—whosoever will, let them come.

Cordelia had been playing this hectic, entrancing game for six months and was widely known among a certain group of young men and girls on the avenue as a fus' class chippie when she and I happened to enter the theatre simultaneously. She had clumped down the aisle before me, her open galoshes swishing noisily, her two arms busy wriggling themselves free from the torn sleeve lining of a shoddy imitation fur coat that one of her mother's wash clients had sent to her. She was of medium height and build, with overly developed legs and bust, and had a clear, keen light brown complexion. Her too slick, too naturally bobbed hair, mussed by the removing of a tight, black turban was of an undecided nature, i.e., it was undecided whether to be kinky or to be kind, and her body, as she sauntered along in the partial light had such a conscious sway of invitation that unthinkingly I followed, slid into the same row of seats and sat down beside her.

Naturally she had noticed my pursuit, and thinking that I was eager to play the game, let me know immediately that she was wise, and not the least bit averse to spooning with me during the evening's performance. Interested, and, I might as well confess, intrigued physically, I too became wise, and played up to her with all the fervor, or so I thought, of an old timer, but Cordelia soon remarked that I was different from mos' of des' sheiks, and when pressed for an explanation brazenly told me in a slightly scandalized and patronizing tone that I had not even felt her legs . . . !

At one o'clock in the morning we strolled through the snowy bleakness of one hundred and forty-fourth street between Lenox and Fifth Avenues to the walk-up tenement flat in which she lived, and after stamping the snow from our feet, pushed through the double outside doors, and followed the dismal hallway to the rear of the building where we began the tedious climbing of the crooked, creaking, inconveniently narrow stairway. Cordelia had informed me earlier in the evening that she lived on the top floor—four flights up east side rear—and on our way we rested at each floor and at each half way landing, rested long enough to mingle the snowy dampness of our respective coats, and to hug clumsily while our lips met in an animal kiss.

Finally only another half flight remained, and instead of proceeding as was usual after our amourous demonstration I abruptly drew away from her, opened my overcoat, plunged my hand into my pants pocket, and drew out two crumpled one dollar bills which I handed to her, and then, while she stared at me foolishly, I muttered good-night, confusedly pecked her on her cold brown cheek, and darted down into the creaking darkness.

~

Six months later I was taking two friends of mine, lately from the provinces, to a Saturday night house-rent party in a well known whore house on one hundred and thirty-fourth street near Lenox Avenue. The place as we entered seemed to be a chaotic riot of raucous noise and clashing color all rhythmically merging in the red, smoke filled room. And there I saw Cordelia savagely careening in a drunken abortion of the Charleston and surrounded by a perspiring circle of handclapping enthusiasts. Finally fatigued, she whirled into an abrupt finish, and stopped so that she stared directly into my face, but being dizzy from the calisthenic turns and the cauterizing liquor she doubted that her eyes recognized someone out of the past, and, visibly trying to sober herself, languidly began to dance a slow drag with a lean hipped pimply faced yellow man who had walked between her and me. At last he released her, and seeing that she was about to leave the room I rushed forward calling Cordelia?—as if I was not yet sure who it was. Stopping in the doorway, she turned to see who had called, and finally recognizing me said simply, without the least trace of emotion,—'Lo kid. . . .

And without another word turned her back and walked into the hall to where she joined four girls standing there. Still eager to speak, I followed and heard one of the girls ask: Who's the dicty kid? . . .

And Cordelia answered: The guy who gimme ma' firs' two bucks. . . .

WALLACE THURMAN.

Color Struck

A Play in Four Scenes

Time: *Twenty years ago and present.*   *Place*: *A Southern City.*

PERSONS

JOHN - - - - - - - - *A light brown-skinned man*
EMMALINE - - - - - - - - - *A black woman*
WESLEY - - - - - - - *A boy who plays an accordion*
EMMALINE'S DAUGHTER - - - - - - *A very white girl*
EFFIE - - - - - - - - - *A mulatto girl*
A RAILWAY CONDUCTOR   A DOCTOR
Several who play mouth organs, guitars, banjos.
Dancers, passengers, etc.

SETTING.—*Early night. The inside of a "Jim Crow" railway coach. The car is parallel to the footlights. The seats on the down stage side of the coach are omitted. There are the luggage racks above the seats. The windows are all open. They are exits in each end of the car—right and left.*

ACTION.—*Before the curtain goes up there is the sound of a locomotive whistle and a stopping engine, loud laughter, many people speaking at once, good-natured shrieks, strumming of stringed instruments, etc. The ascending curtain discovers a happy lot of Negroes boarding the train dressed in the gaudy, twdry best of 1900. They are mostly in couples—each couple bearing a covered-over market basket which the men hastily deposit in the racks as they scramble for seats. There is a litle friendly pushing and shoving. One pair just miss a seat three times, much to the enjoyment of the crowd. Many "plug" silk hats are in evidence, also sun-flowers in button holes. The women are showily dressed in the manner of the time, and quite conscious of their finery. A few seats remain unoccupied.*

*E*nter Effie (*left*) *above, with a basket.* ONE OF THE MEN (*standing, lifting his "plug" in a grand manner*). Howdy do, Miss Effie, you'se lookin' jes lak a rose.

(*Effie blushes and is confused. She looks up and down for a seat.*) Fack is, if you wuzn't walkin' long, ah'd think you *wuz* a rose—(*he looks timidly behind her and the others laugh*). Looka here, where's Sam at?

EFFIE (*tossing her head haughtily*). I don't know an' I don't keer.

THE MAN (*visibly relieved*). Then lemme scorch you to a seat. (*He takes her basket and leads her to a seat center of the car, puts the basket in the rack and seats himself beside her with his hat at a rakish angle.*)

MAN (*sliding his arm along the back of the seat*). How come Sam ain't heah—y'll on a bust?

EFFIE (*angrily*). A man dat don't buy me nothin tuh put in *mah* basket, ain't goin' wid *me* tuh no cake walk. (*The hand on the seat touches her shoulder and she thrusts it away*). Take yo' arms from 'round me, Dinky! Gwan hug yo' Ada!

MAN (*in mock indignation*). Do you think I'd

look at Ada when Ah got a chance tuh be wid you? Ah always wuz sweet on you, but you let ole Mullet-head Sam cut me out.

ANOTHER MAN (*with head out of the window*). Just look at de darkies coming! (*With head insite coach.*) Hey, Dinky! Heah come Ada wid a great big basket.

(*Dinky jumps up from beside Effie and rushes to exit right. In a moment they re-enter and take a seat near entrance. Everyone in coach laughs. Dinky's girl turns and calls back to Effie.*)

GIRL. Where's Sam, Effie?

EFFIE. Lawd knows, Ada.

GIRL. Lawd a mussy! Who you gointer walk de cake wid?

EFFIE. Nobody, Ah reckon. John and Emma gointer win it nohow. They's the bestest cake-walkers in dis state.

ADA. You'se better than Emma any day in de week. Cose Sam cain't walk lake John. (*She stands up and scans the coach.*) Looka heah, ain't John an' Emma going? They ain't on heah!

(*The locomotive bell begins to ring.*)

EFFIE. Mah Gawd, s'pose dey got left!

MAN (*with head out of window*). Heah they come, nip and tuck—whoo-ee! They'se gonna make it! (*He waves excitedly.*) Come on Jawn! (*Everybody crowds the windows, encouraging them by gesture and calls. As the whistle blows twice, and the train begins to move, they enter panting and laughing at left. The only seat left is the one directly in front of Effie.*)

DINKY (*standing*). Don't y'all skeer us no mo' lake dat! There couldn't be no cake walk thout y'all. Dem shad-mouf St. Augustine coons would win dat cake and we would have tuh kill 'em all bodaciously.

JOHN. It was Emmaline nearly made us get left. She says I wuz smiling at Effie on the street car and she had to get off and wait for another one.

EMMA (*removing the hatpins from her hat, turns furiously upon him*). You wuz grinning at her and she wuz grinning back jes lake a ole chessy cat!

JOHN (*positively*). I wuzn't.

EMMA (*about to place her hat in rack*). You wuz. I seen you looking jes lake a possum.

JOHN. I wuzn't. I never gits a chance tuh smile at nobody—you won't let me.

EMMA. Jes the same every time you sees a yaller face, you *takes* a chance. (*They sit down in peeved silence for a minute.*)

DINKY. Ada, les we all sample de basket. I bet you got huckleberry pie.

ADA. No I aint, I got peach an' tater pies, but we aint gonna tetch a thing tell we gits tuh de hall.

DINKY (*mock alarm*). Naw, don't do dat! It's all right tuh save the fried chicken, but pies is *always* et on trains.

ADA. Aw shet up! (*He struggles with her for a kiss. She slaps him but finally yields.*)

JOHN (*looking behind him*). Hellow, Effie, where's Sam?

EFFIE. Deed, I don't know.

JOHN. Y'all on a bust?

EMMA. None ah yo' bizness, you got enough tuh mind yo' own self. Turn 'round!

(*She puts up a pouting mouth and he snatches a kiss. She laughs just as he kisses her again and there is a resounding smack which causes the crowd to laugh. And cries of "Oh you kid!" "Salty dog!"*)

(*Enter conductor left calling tickets cheerfully and laughing at the general merriment.*)

CONDUCTOR. I hope somebody from Jacksonville wins this cake.

JOHN. You live in the "Big Jack?"

CONDUCTOR. Sure do. And I wanta taste a piece of that cake on the way back tonight.

JOHN. Jes rest easy—them Augustiners aint gonna smell it. (*Turns to Emma.*) Is they, baby?

EMMA. Not if Ah kin help it.

Somebody with a guitar sings: "Ho babe, mah honey taint no lie."

(*The conductor takes up tickets, passes on and exits right.*)

WESLEY. Look heah, you cake walkers—y'all oughter git up and limber up yo' joints. I heard them folks over to St. Augustine been oiling up wid goose-grease, and over to Ocala they been rubbing down in snake oil.

A WOMAN'S VOICE. You better shut up, Wesley, you just joined de church last month. Somebody's going to tell the pastor on you.

WESLEY. Tell it, tell it, take it up and smell it. Come on out you John and Emma and Effie, and limber up.

JOHN. Naw, we don't wanta do our walking steps—nobody won't wanta see them when we step out at the hall. But we kin do something else just to warm ourselves up.

(*Wesley begins to play "Goo Goo Eyes" on his accordian, the other instruments come in one by one and John and Emma step into the aisle and "parade" up and down the aisle—Emma holding up her skirt, showing the lace on her petticoats. They two-step back to their seat amid much applause.*)

WESLEY. Come on out, Effie! Sam aint heah so you got to hold up his side too. Step on out. (*There is a murmur of applause as she steps into the aisle. Wesley strikes up "I'm gointer live anyhow till I die." It is played quite spiritedly as Effie swings into the pas-me-la—*)

WESLEY (*in ecstasy*). Hot stuff I reckon! Hot stuff I reckon! (*The musicians are stamping. Great enthusiasm. Some clap time with hands and feet. She hurls herself into a modified Hoochy Koochy, and finishes up with an ecstatic yell.*)

There is a babble of talk and laughter and exultation.

JOHN (*applauding loudly*). If dat Effie can't step nobody can.

EMMA. Course you'd say so cause it's her. Everything she do is pretty to you.

JOHN (*caressing her*). Now don't say that, Honey. Dancing is dancing no matter who is doing it. But nobody can hold a candle to you in nothing.

(*Some men are heard tuning up—getting pitch to sing. Four of them crowd together in one seat and begin the chorus of "Daisies Won't Tell." John and Emma grow quite affectionate.*)

JOHN (*kisses her*). Emma, what makes you always picking a fuss with me over some yaller girl.

What makes you so jealous, nohow ? I don't do nothing.

(*She clings to him, but he turns slightly away. The train whistle blows, there is a slackening of speed. Passengers begin to take down baskets from their racks.*)

EMMA. John! John, don't you want me to love you, honey?

JOHN (*turns and kisses her slowly*). Yes, I want you to love me, you know I do. But I don't like to be accused o' ever light colored girl in the world. It hurts my feeling. I don't want to be jealous like you are.

(*Enter at right Conductor, crying "St. Augus-* tine, St. Augustine." *He exits left. The crowd has congregated at the two exits, pushing good-na- turedly and joking. All except John and Emma. They are still seated with their arms about each other.*)

EMMA (*sadly*). Then you don't want my love, John, cause I can't help mahself from being jealous. I loves you so hard, John, and jealous love is the only kind I got.

(*John kisses her very feelingly.*)

EMMA. Just for myself alone is the only way I knows how to love.

(*They are standing in the aisle with their arms about each other as the curtain falls.*)

SCENE II

SETTING.—*A weather-board hall. A large room with the joists bare. The place has been divided by a curtain of sheets stretched and a rope across from left to right. From behind the curtain there are occasional sounds of laughter, a note or two on a stringed instrument or accordion. General stir. That is the dance hall. The front is the ante-room where the refreshments are being served. A "plank" seat runs all around the hall, along the walls. The lights are kero- sene lamps with reflectors. They are fixed to the wall. The lunch-baskets are under the seat. There is a table on either side upstage with a woman behind each. At one, ice cream is sold, at the other, roasted peanuts and large red- and-white sticks of peppermint candy.*

People come in by twos and three, laughing, joking, horse-plays, gauchily flowered dresses, small waists, bulging hips and busts, hats worn far back on the head, etc. People from Ocala greet others from Palatka, Jacksonville, St. Augustine, etc.

Some find seats in the ante-room, others pass on into the main hall.

Enter the Jacksonville delegation, laughing, pushing proudly.

DINKY. Here we is, folks—here we *is*. Gointer take dat cake on back tuh Jacksonville where it be- longs.

MAN. Gwan! Whut wid you mullet-head Jacksonville Coons know whut to do wid a cake. It's gointer stay right here in Augustine where de *good* cake walkers grow.

DINKY. Taint no 'Walkers' never walked till John and Emmaline prance out—you mighty come a tootin'.

Great laughing and joshing as more people come in. John and Emma are encouraged, urged on to win.

EMMA. Let's we git a seat, John, and set down.

JOHN. Sho will—nice one right over there. (*They push over to wall seat, place basket under- neath, and sit. Newcomers shake hands with them and urge them on to win.*)

(*Enter Joe Clarke and a small group. He is a rotund, expansive man with a liberal watch chain and charm.*)

DINKY (*slapping Clarke on the back*). If you don't go 'way from here! Lawdy, if it aint Joe.

CLARKE (*jovially*). Ah thought you had done forgot us people in Eatonville since you been living up here in Jacksonville.

DINKY. Course Ah aint. (*Turning.*) Looka heah folks! Joe Clarke oughta be made chairman uh dis meetin'—Ah mean Past Great-Grand Mas- ter of Ceremonies, him being the onliest mayor of de onliest colored town in de state.

GENERAL CHORUS. Yeah, let him be—thass fine, etc.

DINKY (*setting his hat at a new angle and throw- ing out his chest*). And *Ah'll* scorch him to de platform. Ahem!

(*Sprinkling of laughter as Joe Clarke is escorted into next room by Dinky.*)

(*The musicians are arriving one by one during this time. A guitar, accordian, mouth organ, banjo, etc. Soon there is a rapping for order heard inside and the voice of Joe Clarke.*)

JOE CLARKE. Git yo' partners one an' all for de gran' march! Git yo' partners, gent-mens!

A MAN (*drawing basket from under bench*). Let's we all eat first.

(*John and Emma go buy ice-cream. They coquettishly eat from each other's spoons. Old Man Lizzimore crosses to Effie and removes his hat and bows with a great flourish.*)

LIZZIMORE. Sam ain't here t'night, is he, Effie.

EFFIE (*embarrassed*). Naw suh, he aint.

LIZZ. Well, you like chicken? (*Extends arm to her.*) Take a wing!

(*He struts her up to the table amid the laughter of the house. He wears no collar.*)

JOHN (*squeezes Emma's hand*). You certainly is a ever loving mamma—when you aint mad.

EMMA (*smiles sheepishly*). You oughtn't to make me mad then.

JOHN. Ah don't make you! You makes yo'self mad, den blame it on me. Ah keep on tellin' you Ah don't love nobody but you. Ah knows heaps uh half-white girls Ah could git ef Ah wanted to. But (*he squeezes her hard again*) Ah jus' wants *you!* You know what they say! De darker de berry, de sweeter de taste!

EMMA (*pretending to pout*). Oh, you tries to run over me an' keep it under de cover, but Ah won't let yuh. (*Both laugh.*) Les' we eat our basket!

JOHN. Alright. (*He pulls the basket out and she removes the table cloth. They set the basket on their knees and begin to eat fried chicken.*)

MALE VOICE. Les' everybody eat—motion's done carried. (*Everybody begins to open baskets. All have fried chicken. Very good humor prevails. Delicacies are swapped from one basket to the other. John and Emma offer the man next them some supper. He takes a chicken leg. Effie crosses to John and Emma with two pieces of pie on a plate.*)

EFFIE. Y'll have a piece uh mah blueberry pie —it's mighty nice! (*She proffers it with a timid smile to Emma who "freezes" up instantly.*)

EMMA. Naw! We don't want no pie. We got cocoanut layer-cake.

JOHN. Ah—Ah think ah'd choose a piece uh pie, Effie. (*He takes it.*) Will you set down an' have a snack wid us? (*He slides over to make room.*)

EFFIE (*nervously*). Ah, naw, Ah got to run on back to mah basket, but Ah thought maybe y'll mout' want tuh taste mah pie. (*She turns to go.*)

JOHN. Thank you, Effie. It's mighty good, too. (*He eats it. Effie crosses to her seat. Emma glares at her for a minute, then turns disgustedly away from the basket. John catches her shoulder and faces her around.*)

JOHN (*pleadingly*). Honey, be nice. Don't act lak dat!

EMMA (*jerking free*). Naw, you done ruint mah appetite now, carryin' on wid dat punkin-colored ole gal.

JOHN. Whut kin Ah do? If you had a acted polite Ah wouldn't a had nothin' to say.

EMMA. Naw, youse jus' hog-wile ovah her cause she's half-white! No matter whut Ah say, you keep carryin' on wid her. Act polite? Naw Ah aint gonna be deceitful an' bust mah gizzard fuh nobody! Let her keep her dirty ole pie ovah there where she is!

JOHN (*looking around to see if they are overheard*). Sh-sh! Honey, you mustn't talk so loud.

EMMA (*louder*). Ah-Ah aint gonna bite mah tongue! If she don't like it she can lump it. Mah back is broad—(*John tries to cover her mouth with his hand*). She calls herself a big cigar, but *I* kin smoke her!

(*The people are laughing and talking for the most part and pay no attention. Effie is laughing and talking to those around her and does not hear the tirade. The eating is over and everyone is going behind the curtain. John and Emma put away their basket like the others, and sit glum. Voice of Master-of-ceremonies can be heard from beyond curtain announcing the pas-me-la contest. The contestants, mostly girls, take the floor. There is no music except the clapping of hands and the shouts of "Parse-me-lah" in time with the hand-clapping. At the end Master announces winner. Shadows seen on curtain.*)

MASTER. Mathilda Clarke is winner—if she will step forward she will receive a beautiful wook fascinator. (*The girl goes up and receives it with great hand-clapping and good humor.*) And now since the roosters is crowin' foah midnight, an' most of us got to git up an' go to work tomorrow, The Great Cake Walk will begin. Ah wants de floor cleared, cause de representatives of de several cities will be announced an' we wants 'em to take de floor as their names is called. Den we wants 'em to do a gran' promenade roun' de hall. An' they will then commence to walk fuh de biggest cake ever baked in dis state. Ten dozen eggs—ten pounds of flour —ten pounds of butter, and so on and so forth.

Now then—(*he strikes a pose*) for St. Augustine—
Miss Lucy Taylor, Mr. Ned Coles.
(*They step out amid applause and stand before stage.*)
For Daytona—
Miss Janie Bradley, Enoch Nixon
(*Same business.*)
For Ocala—
Miss Docia Boger, Mr. Oscar Clarke
(*Same business.*)
For Palatka—
Miss Maggie Lemmons, Mr. Senator Lewis
(*Same business.*)
And for Jacksonville the most popular "walkers" in de state—
Miss Emmaline Beazeby, Mr. John Turner.
(*Tremendous applause. John rises and offers his arm grandiloquently to Emma.*)
EMMA (*pleadingly, and clutching his coat*). John let's we all don't go in there with all them. Let's we all go on home.
JOHN (*amazed*). Why, Emma?
EMMA. Cause, cause all them girls is going to pulling and hauling on you, and—
JOHN (*impatiently*). Shucks! Come on. Don't you hear the people clapping for us and calling our names? Come on!
(*He tries to pull her up—she tries to drag him back.*)
Come on, Emma! Taint no sense in your acting like this. The band is playing for us. Hear 'em? (*He moves feet in a dance step.*)
EMMA. Naw, John, Ah'm skeered. I loves you —I—.
(*He tries to break away from her. She is holding on fiercely.*)

JOHN. I got to go! I been practising almost a year—I—we done come all the way down here. I can walk the cake, Emma—we got to—I got to go in! (*He looks into her face and sees her tremendous fear.*) What you skeered about?
EMMA (*hopefully*). You won't go it—You'll come on go home with me all by ourselves. Come on John. I can't, I just can't go in there and see all them girls—Effie hanging after you—.
JOHN. I got to go in—(*he removes her hand from his coat*)—whether you come with me or not.
EMMA. Oh—them yaller wenches! How I hate 'em! They gets everything they wants—.
VOICE INSIDE. We are waiting for the couple from Jacksonville—Jacksonville! Where is the couple from—.
(*Wesley parts the curtain and looks out.*)
WESLEY. Here they is out here spooning! You all can't even hear your names called. Come on John and Emma.
JOHN. Coming. (*He dashes inside. Wesley stands looking at Emma in surprise.*)
WESLEY. What's the matter, Emma? You and John spatting again? (*He goes back inside.*)
EMMA (*calmly bitter*). He went and left me. If we is spatting we done had our last one. (*She stands and clenches her fists.*) Ah, mah God! He's in there with her—Oh, them half whites, they gets everything, they gets everything everybody else wants! The men, the jobs—everything! The whole world is got a sign on it. Wanted: Light colored. Us blacks was made for cobble stones. (*She muffles a cry and sinks limp upon the seat.*)
VOICE INSIDE. Miss Effie Jones will walk for Jacksonville with Mr. John Turner in place of Miss Emmaline Beazeley.

SCENE III—*Dance Hall*
Emma springs to her feet and flings the curtains wide open. She stands staring at the gay scene for a moment defiantly ,then creeps over to a seat along the wall and shrinks into the Spanish Moss, motionless.
Dance hall decorated with palmetto leaves and Spanish Moss—a flag or two.
Orchestra consists of guitar, mandolin, banjo, accordian, church organ and drum.

MASTER (*on platform*). Couples take yo' places! When de music starts, gentlemen parade yo' ladies once round de hall, den de walk begins. (*The music begins. Four men come out from behind the platform bearing a huge chocolate cake. The couples are "prancing" in their tracks. The men lead off the procession with the cake—the contestants make a grand slam around the hall.*)
MASTER. Couples to de floor! Stan' back, ladies an' gentlemen—give 'em plenty room.

(*Music changes to "Way Down in Georgia." Orchestra sings. Effie takes the arm that John offers her and they parade to the other end of the hall. She takes her place. John goes back upstage to the platform, takes off his silk hat in a graceful sweep as he bows deeply to Effie. She lifts her skirts and curtsies to the floor. Both smile broadly. They advance toward each other, meet midway, then, arm in arm, begin to "strut." John falters as he faces her, but recovers promptly and is perfection in his style.* (*Seven to nine minutes to curtain.*) *Fervor of spectators grows until all are taking part in some way—either hand-clapping or singing the words. At curtain they have reached frenzy.*)

QUICK CURTAIN

(*It stays down a few seconds to indicate ending of contest and goes up again on John and Effie being declared winners by Judges.*)

MASTER (*on platform, with John and Effie on the floor before him*). By unanimous decision de cake goes to de couple from Jacksonville! (*Great enthusiasm. The cake is set down in the center of the floor and the winning couple parade around it arm in arm. John and Effie circle the cake happily* and triumphantly. *The other contestants, and then the entire assembly fall in behind and circle the cake, singing and clapping. The festivities continue. The Jacksonville quartet step upon the platform and sing a verse and chorus of "Daisies won't tell." Cries of "Hurrah for Jacksonville! Glory for the big town," "Hurrah for Big Jack."*)

A MAN (*seeing Emma*). You're from Jacksonville, aint you? (*He whirls her around and around.*) Aint you happy? Whoopee! (*He releases her and she drops upon a seat. She buries her face in the moss.*)

(*Quartet begins on chorus again. People are departing, laughing, humming, with quartet cheering. John, the cake, and Effie being borne away in triumph.*)

SCENE IV

Time—present. The interior of a one-room shack in an alley. There is a small window in the rear wall upstage left. There is an enlarged crayon drawing of a man and woman—man sitting cross-legged, woman standing with her hand on his shoulder. A center table, red cover, a low, cheap rocker, two straight chairs, a small kitchen stove at left with a wood-box beside it, a water-bucket on a stand close by. A hand towel and a wash basin. A shelf of dishes above this. There is an ordinary oil lamp on the center table but it is not lighted when the curtain goes up. Some light enters through the window and falls on the woman seated in the low rocker. The door is center right. A cheap bed is against the upstage wall. Someone is on the bed but is lying so that the back is toward the audience.

Action—As the curtain rises, the woman is seen rocking to and fro in the low rocker. A dead silence except for the sound of the rocker and an occasional groan from the bed. Once a faint voice says "water" and the woman in the rocker arises and carries the tin dipper to the bed.

WOMAN. No mo' right away—Doctor says not too much. (*Returns dipper to pail.—Pause.*) You got right much fever—I better go git the doctor agin.

(*There comes a knocking at the door and she stands still for a moment, listening. It comes again and she goes to door but does not open it.*)

WOMAN. Who's that?

VOICE OUTSIDE. Does Emma Beasely live here?

EMMA. Yeah—(*pause*)—who is it?

VOICE. It's me—John Turner.

EMMA (*puts hands eagerly on the fastening*). John? did you say John Turner?

VOICE. Yes, Emma, it's me.

(*The door is opened and the man steps inside.*)

EMMA. John! Your hand (*she feels for it and touches it*). John flesh and blood.

JOHN (*laughing awkwardly*). It's me alright, old girl. Just as bright as a basket of chips. Make a light quick so I can see how you look. I'm crazy to see you. Twenty years is a long time to wait, Emma.

EMMA (*nervously*). Oh, let's we all just sit in the dark awhile. (*Apologetically.*) I wasn't expecting nobody and my house aint picked up. Sit down. (*She draws up the chair. She sits in rocker.*)

JOHN. Just to think! Emma! Me and Emma sitting down side by each. Know how I found you?

EMMA (*dully*). Naw. How?

JOHN (*brightly*). Soon's I got in town I hunted up Wesley and he told me how to find you. That's who I come to see, you!

EMMA. Where you been all these years, up North somewheres? Nobody round here could find out where you got to.

JOHN. Yes, up North. Philadelphia.

EMMA. Married yet?

JOHN. Oh yes, seventeen years ago. But my wife is dead now and so I came as soon as it was decent to find *you*. I wants to marry you. I couldn't die happy if I didn't. Couldn't get over you—couldn't forget. Forget me, Emma?

EMMA. Naw, John. How could I?

JOHN (*leans over impulsively to catch her hand*). Oh, Emma, I love you so much. Strike a light honey so I can see you—see if you changed much. You was such a handsome girl!

EMMA. We don't exactly need no light, do we, John, tuh jus' set an' talk?

JOHN. Yes, we do, Honey. Gwan, make a light. Ah wanna see you.

(*There is a silence.*)

EMMA. Bet you' wife wuz some high-yaller dickty-doo.

JOHN. Naw she wasn't neither. She was jus' as much like you as Ah could get her. Make a light an' Ah'll show you her pictcher. Shucks, ah gotta look at mah old sweetheart. (*He strikes a match and holds it up between their faces and they look intently at each other over it until it burns out.*) You aint changed none atall, Emma, jus' as pretty as a speckled pup yet.

EMMA (*lighter*). Go long, John! (*Short pause*) 'member how you useter bring me magnolias?

JOHN. Do I? Gee, you was sweet! 'Member how Ah useter pull mah necktie loose so you could tie it back for me? Emma, Ah can't see to mah soul how we lived all this time, way from one another. 'Member how you useter make out mah ears had done run down and you useter screw 'em up agin for me? (*They laugh.*)

EMMA. Yeah, Ah useter think you wuz gointer be mah husban' then—but you let dat ole—.

JOHN. Ah aint gonna let you alibi on me lak dat. Light dat lamp! You cain't look me in de eye and say no such. (*He strikes another match and lights the lamp.*) Course, Ah don't wanta look too bossy, but Ah b'lieve you got to marry me tuh git rid of me. That is, if you aint married.

EMMA. Naw, Ah aint. (*She turns the lamp down.*)

JOHN (*looking about the room*). Not so good, Emma. But wait till you see dat little place in Philly! Got a little "Rolls-Rough," too—gointer teach you to drive it, too.

EMMA. Ah been havin' a hard time, John, an' Ah lost you—oh, aint nothin' been right for me! Ah aint never been happy.

(*John takes both of her hands in his.*)

JOHN. You gointer be happy now, Emma. Cause Ah'm gointer make you. Gee Whiz! Ah aint but forty-two and you aint forty yet—we got plenty time. (*There is a groan from the bed.*) Gee, what's that?

EMMA (*ill at ease*). Thass mah chile. She's sick. Reckon Ah bettah see 'bout her.

JOHN. You got a chile? Gee, that great! Ah always wanted one. but didn't have no luck. Now we kin start off with a family. Girl or boy?

EMMA (*slowly*). A girl. Comin' tuh see me agin soon, John?

JOHN. Comin' agin? Ah aint gone yet! We aint talked, you aint kissed me an' nothin', and you aint showed me our girl. (*Another groan, more prolonged.*) She must be pretty sick—let's see. (*He turns in his chair and Emma rushes over to the bed and covers the girl securely, tucking her long hair under the covers, too—before he arises. He goes over to the bed and looks down into her face. She is mulatto. Turns to Emma teasingly.*) Talkin' 'bout *me* liking high-yallers—yo husband musta been pretty near *white.*

EMMA (*slowly*). Ah, never wuz married, John.

JOHN. It's alright, Emma. (*Kisses her warmly.*) Everything is going to be O.K. (*Turning back to the bed.*) Our child looks pretty sick, but she's pretty. (*Feels her forehead and cheek.*) Think she oughter have a doctor.

EMMA. Ah done had one. Course Ah cain't git no specialist an' nothin' lak dat. (*She looks about the room and his gaze follows hers.*) Ah aint got a whole lot lake you. Nobody don't git rich in no white-folks' kitchen, nor in de washtub. You know Ah aint no school-teacher an' nothin' lak dat.

(*John puts his arm about her.*)

JOHN. It's all right, Emma. But our daughter is bad off—run out an' git a doctor—she needs one. Ah'd go if Ah knowed where to find one—you kin git one the quickest—hurry, Emma.

EMMA (*looks from John to her daughter and back again.*) She'll be all right, Ah reckon, for a while. John, you love me—you really want me sho' nuff?

JOHN. Sure Ah do—think Ah'd come all de way down here for nothin'? Ah wants to marry agin.

EMMA. Soon, John?

JOHN. Real soon.

EMMA. Ah wuz jus' thinkin', mah folks is away now on a little trip—be home day after tomorrow—we could git married tomorrow.

JOHN. All right. Now run on after the doctor—we must look after our girl. Gee, she's got a full suit of hair! Glad you didn't let her chop it off. (*Looks away from bed and sees Emma standing still.*)

JOHN. Emma, run on after the doctor, honey. (*She goes to the bed and again tucks the long braids of hair in, which are again pouring over the side of the bed by the feverish tossing of the girl.*)   What's our daughter's name?

EMMA. Lou Lillian. (*She returns to the rocker uneasily and sits rocking jerkily. He returns to his seat and turns up the light.*)

JOHN. Gee, we're going to be happy—we gointer make up for all them twenty years (*another groan*). Emma, git up an' gwan git dat doctor. You done forgot Ah'm de boss uh dis family now—gwan, while Ah'm here to watch her whilst you're gone. Ah got to git back to mah stoppin'-place after a while.

EMMA. You go git one, John.

JOHN. Whilst Ah'm blunderin' round tryin' to find one, she'll be gettin' worse. She sounds pretty bad—(*takes out his wallet and hands her a bill*)—get a taxi if necessary. Hurry!

EMMA (*does not take the money, but tucks her arms and hair in again, and gives the girl a drink*). Reckon Ah better go git a doctor. Don't want nothin' to happen to *her.* After you left, Ah useter have such a hurtin' in heah (*touches bosom*) till she come an' eased it some.

JOHN. Here, take some money and get a good doctor. There must be some good colored ones around here now.

EMMA (*scornfully*). I wouldn't let one of 'em tend my cat if I had one! But let's we don't start a fuss.

(*John caresses her again. When he raises his head he notices the picture on the wall and crosses over to it with her—his arm still about her.*)

JOHN. Why, that's you and me!

EMMA. Yes, I never could part with that. You coming tomorrow morning, John, and we're gointer get married, aint we? Then we can talk over everything.

JOHN. Sure, but I aint gone yet. I don't see how come we can't make all our arrangements now.

(*Groans from bed and feeble movement.*)

Good lord, Emma, go get that doctor!

(*Emma stares at the girl and the bed and seizes a hat from a nail on the wall. She prepares to go but looks from John to bed and back again. She fumbles about the table and lowers the lamp. Goes to door and opens it. John offers the wallet. She refuses it.*)

EMMA. Doctor right around the corner. Guess I'll leave the door open so she can get some air. She won't need nothing while I'm gone, John. (*She crosses and tucks the girl in securely and rushes out, looking backward and pushing the door wide open as she exits. John sits in the chair beside the table. Looks about him—shakes his head. The girl on*

the bed groans, "water," "so hot." *John looks about him excitedly. Gives her a drink. Feels her forehead. Takes a clean handkerchief from his pocket and wets it and places it upon her forehead. She raises her hand to the cool object. Enter Emma running. When she sees John at the bed she is full of fury. She rushes over and jerks his shoulder around. They face each other.*)

EMMA. I knowed it! (*She strikes him.*) A half white skin. (*She rushes at him again. John staggers back and catches her hands.*)

JOHN. Emma!

EMMA (*struggles to free her hands*). Let me go so I can kill you. Come sneaking in here like a pole cat!

JOHN (*slowly, after a long pause*). So this is the woman I've been wearing over my heart like a rose for twenty years! She so despises her own skin that she can't believe any one else could love it!

(*Emma writhes to free herself.*)

JOHN. Twenty years! Twenty years of adoration, of hunger, of worship! (*On the verge of tears he crosses to door and exits quietly, closing the door after him.*)

(*Emma remains standing, looking dully about as if she is half asleep. There comes a knocking at the door. She rushes to open it. It is the doctor. White. She does not step aside so that he can enter.*)

DOCTOR. Well, shall I come in?

EMMA (*stepping aside and laughing a little*). That's right, doctor, come in.

(*Doctor crosses to bed with professional air. Looks at the girl, feels the pulse and draws up the sheet over the face. He turns to her.*)

DOCTOR. Why didn't you come sooner. I told you to let me know of the least change in her condition.

EMMA (*flatly*). I did come—I went for the doctor.

DOCTOR. Yes, but you waited. An hour more or less is mighty important sometimes. Why didn't you come?

EMMA (*passes hand over face*). Couldn't see.

(*Doctor looks at her curiously, then sympathetically takes out a small box of pills, and hands them to her.*) Here, you're worn out. Take one of these every hour and try to get some sleep. (*He departs.*)

(*She puts the pill-box on the table, takes up the low rocking chair and places it by the head of the bed. She seats herself and rocks monotonously and stares out of the door. A dry sob now and then. The wind from the open door blows out the lamp and she is seen by the little light from the window rocking in an even, monotonous gait, and sobbing.*)

Flame From the Dark Tower

A Section of Poetry

From the Dark Tower

We shall not always plant while others reap
The golden increment of bursting fruit,
Nor always countenance, abject and mute,
That lesser men should hold their brothers cheap;
Not everlastingly while others sleep
Shall we beguile their limbs with mellow flute,
Not always bend to some more subtle brute;
We were not made eternally to weep.

The night whose sable breast relieves the stark,
White stars is no less lovely being dark,
And there are buds that cannot bloom at all
In light, but crumple, piteous, and fall.
So in the dark we hide the heart that bleeds,
And wait, and tend our agonizing seeds.

COUNTÉE CULLEN.

A Southern Road

Yolk-colored tongue
    Parched beneath a burning sky,
    A lazy little tune
    Hummed up the crest of some
    Soft sloping hill.
    One streaming line of beauty
    Flowing by a forest
    Pregnant with tears.
    A hidden nest for beauty
    Idly flung by God
    In one lonely lingering hour
    Before the Sabbath.
    A blue-fruited black gum,
    Like a tall predella,
    Bears a dangling figure,—
    Sacrificial dower to the raff,
    Swinging alone,
    A solemn, tortured shadow in the air.

             HELENE JOHNSON.

Jungle Taste

There is a coarseness
In the songs of black men
Coarse as the songs
Of the sea.
There is a weird strangeness
In the songs of black men
Which sounds not strange
To me.

There is beauty
In the faces of black women,
Jungle beauty
And mystery.
Dark, hidden beauty
In the faces of black women
Which only black men
See.

Finality

Trees are the souls of men
Reaching skyward.
And while each soul
Draws nearer God
Its dark roots cleave
To earthly sod:
    Death, only death
    Brings triumph to the soul.
    The silent grave alone
    Can bare the goal.
    Then roots and all
    Must lie forgot—
    To rot.

EDWARD SILVERA.

The Death Bed

All the time they were praying
He watched the shadow of a tree
Flicker on the wall.

There is no need of prayer.
He said,
No need at all.

The kin-folk thought it strange
That he should ask them from a dying bed.
But they left all in a row
And it seemed to ease him
To see them go.

There were some who kept on praying
In a room across the hall
And some who listened to the breeze
That made the shadows waver
On the wall.

He tried his nerve
On a song he knew
And made an empty note
That might have come,
From a bird's harsh throat.

And all the time it worried him
That they were in there praying
And all the time he wondered
What it was they could be saying.

WARING CUNEY.

Elevator Boy

I got a job now
Runnin' an elevator
In the Dennison Hotel in Jersey,
Job aint no good though.
No money around.
    Jobs are just chances
    Like everything else.
    Maybe a little luck now,
    Maybe not.
    Maybe a good job sometimes:
    Step out o' the barrel, boy.
Two new suits an'
A woman to sleep with.
    Maybe no luck for a long time.
    Only the elevators
    Goin' up an' down,
    Up an' down,
    Or somebody else's shoes
    To shine,
    Or greasy pots in a dirty kitchen.
I been runnin' this
Elevator too long.
Guess I'll quit now.

LANGSTON HUGHES.

Railroad Avenue

Dusk dark
On Railroad Avenue.
Lights in the fish joints,
Lights in the pool rooms.
A box car some train
Has forgotten
In the middle of the block.
A player piano,
A victrola.
    942
     Was the number.
A boy
Lounging on the corner.
A passing girl
With purple powdered skin.
    Laughter
    Suddenly
    Like a taut drum.
    Laughter
    Suddenly
    Neither truth nor lie.
    Laughter
Hardening the dusk dark evening.
    Laughter
Shaking the lights in the fish joints,
Rolling white balls in the pool rooms,
And leaving untouched the box car
Some train has forgotten.

                    LANGSTON HUGHES.

Length of Moon

Then the golden hour
Will tick its last
And the flame will go down in the flower.

A briefer length of moon
Will mark the sea-line and the yellow dune.

Then we may think of this, yet
There will be something forgotten
And something we should forget.

It will be like all things we know:
A stone will fail; a rose is sure to go.

It will be quiet then and we may stay
Long at the picket gate,—
But there will be less to say.

ARNA BONTEMPS.

Little Cinderella

ook me over, kid!
I knows I'm neat,—
Little Cinderella from head to feet.
Drinks all night at Club Alabam,—
What comes next I don't give a damn!

Daddy, daddy,
You sho' looks keen!
I likes men that are long and lean.
Broad Street ain't got no brighter lights
Than your eyes at pitch midnight.

Streets

Avenues of dreams
Boulevards of pain
Moving black streams
Shimmering like rain.

LEWIS ALEXANDER.

Wedding Day

His name was Paul Watson and as he shambled down rue Pigalle he might have been any other Negro of enormous height and size. But as I have said, his name was Paul Watson. Passing him on the street, you might not have known or cared who he was, but any one of the residents about the great Montmartre district of Paris could have told you who he was as well as many interesting bits of his personal history.

He had come to Paris in the days before colored jazz bands were the style. Back home he had been a prize fighter. In the days when Joe Gans was in his glory Paul was following the ring, too. He didn't have that fine way about him that Gans had and for that reason luck seemed to go against him. When he was in the ring he was like a mad bull, especially if his opponent was a white man. In those days there wasn't any sympathy or nicety about the ring and so pretty soon all the ringmasters got down on Paul and he found it pretty hard to get a bout with anyone. Then it was that he worked his way across the Atlantic Ocean on a big liner—in the days before colored jazz bands were the style in Paris.

Things flowed along smoothly for the first few years with Paul's working here and there in the unfrequented places of Paris. On the side he used to give boxing lessons to aspiring youths or gymnastic young women. At that time he was working so steadily that he had little chance to find out what was going on around Paris. Pretty soon, however, he grew to be known among the trainers and managers began to fix up bouts for him. After one or two successful bouts a little fame began to come into being for him. So it was that after one of the prize-fights, a colored fellow came to his dressing room to congratulate him on his success as well as invite him to go to Montmartre to meet "the boys."

Paul had a way about him and seemed to get on with the colored fellows who lived in Montmartre and when the first Negro jazz band played in a tiny Parisian cafe Paul was among them playing the banjo. Those first years were without event so far as Paul was concerned. The members of that first band often say now that they wonder how it was that nothing happened during those first seven years, for it was generally known how great was Paul's hatred for American white people. I suppose the tranquility in the light of what happened afterwards was due to the fact that the cafe in which they worked was one in which mostly French people drank and danced and then too, that was before there were so many Americans visiting Paris. However, everyone had heard Paul speak of his intense hatred of American white folks. It only took two Benedictines to make him start talking about what he would do to the first "Yank" that called him "nigger." But the seven years came to an end and Paul Watson went to work in a larger cafe with a larger band, patronized almost solely by Americans.

I've heard almost every Negro in Montmartre tell about the night that a drunken Kentuckian came into the cafe where Paul was playing and said:

"Look heah, Bruther, what you all doin' ovah heah?"

"None ya bizness. And looka here, I ain't your brother, see?"

"Jack, do you heah that nigger talkin' lak that tah me?"

As he said this, he turned to speak to his companion. I have often wished that I had been there to have seen the thing happen myself. Every tale I have heard about it was different and yet there was something of truth in each of them. Perhaps the nearest one can come to the truth is by saying that Paul beat up about four full-sized white men that night besides doing a great deal of damage to the furniture about the cafe. I couldn't tell you just what did happen. Some of the fellows say that Paul seized the nearest table and mowed down men right and left, others say he took a bottle, then again the story runs that a chair was the instrument of his fury. At any rate, that started Paul Watson on his seige against the American white person who brings his native prejudices into the life of Paris.

It is a verity that Paul was the "black terror." The last syllable of the word, nigger, never passed the lips of a white man without the quick reflex action of Paul's arm and fist to the speaker's jaw. He paid for more glassware and cafe furnishings in the course of the next few years than is easily imaginable. And yet, there was something likable about Paul. Perhaps that's the reason that he stood in so well with the policemen of the neighborhood. Always some divine power seemed to intervene in his behalf and he was excused after the payment of a small fine with advice about his future conduct. Finally, there came the night when in a frenzy he shot the two American sailors.

They had not died from the wounds he had given them hence his sentence had not been one of death but rather a long term of imprisonment. It was a pitiable sight to see Paul sitting in the corner of his cell with his great body hunched almost double. He seldom talked and when he did his words were interspersed with oaths about the lowness of "crackers." Then the World War came.

It seems strange that anything so horrible as that wholesale slaughter could bring about any good and yet there was something of a smoothing quality about even its baseness. There has never been such equality before or since such as that which the World War brought. Rich men fought by the side of paupers; poets swapped yarns with dry-goods salesmen, while Jews and Christians ate corned beef out of the same tin. Along with the general leveling influence came France's pardon of her prisoners in order that they might enter the army. Paul Watson became free and a French soldier. Because he was strong and had innate daring in his heart he was placed in the aerial squad and cited many times for bravery. The close of the war gave him his place in French society as a hero. With only a memory of the war and an ugly scar on his left cheek he took up his old life.

His firm resolutions about American white people still remained intact and many chance encounters that followed the war are told from lip to lip proving that the war and his previous imprisonment had changed him little. He was the same Paul Watson to Montmartre as he shambled up rue Pigalle.

Rue Pigalle in the early evening has a sombre beauty—gray as are most Paris streets and otherworldish. To those who know the district it is the Harlem of Paris and rue Pigalle is its dusky Seventh Avenue. Most of the colored musicians that furnish Parisians and their visitors with entertainment live somewhere in the neighborhood of rue Pigalle. Some time during every day each of these musicians makes a point of passing through rue Pigalle. Little wonder that almost any day will find Paul Watson going his shuffling way up the same street.

He reached the corner of rue de la Bruyere and with sure instinct his feet stopped. Without half thinking he turned into "the Pit." Its full name is The Flea Pit. If you should ask one of the musicians why it was so called, he would answer you to the effect that it was called "the pit" because all the "fleas" hang out there. If you did not get the full import of this explanation, he would go further and say that there were always "spades" in the pit and they were as thick as fleas. Unless

you could understand this latter attempt at clarity you could not fully grasp what the Flea-Pit means to the Negro musicians in Montmartre. It is a tiny cafe of the genus that is called *bistro* in France. Here the fiddle players, saxophone blowers, drumbeaters and ivory ticklers gather at four in the afternoon for a porto or a game of billiards. Here the cabaret entertainers and supper musicians meet at one o'clock at night or thereafter for a whiskey and soda, or more billiards. Occasional sandwiches and a "quiet game" also play their parts in the popularity of the place. After a season or two it becomes a settled fact just what time you may catch so-and-so at the famous "Pit."

The musicians were very fond of Paul and took particular delight in teasing him. He was one of the chosen few that all of the musicians conceded as being "regular." It was the pet joke of the habitues of the cafe that Paul never bothered with girls. They always said that he could beat up ten men but was scared to death of one woman.

"Say fellow, when ya goin' a get hooked up?"

"Can't say, Bo. Ain't so much on skirts."

"Man alive, ya don't know what you're missin' —somebody little and cute telling ya sweet things in your ear. Paris is full of women folks."

"I ain't much on 'em all the same. Then too, they're all white."

"What's it to ya? This ain't America."

"Can't help that. Get this—I'm collud, see? I ain't got nothing for no white meat to do. If a woman eva called me nigger I'd have to kill her, that's all!"

"You for it, son. I can't give you a thing on this Mr. Jefferson Lawd way of lookin' at women."

"Oh, tain't that. I guess they're all right for those that wants 'em. Not me!"

"Oh you ain't so forty. You'll fall like all the other spades I've ever seen. Your kind falls hardest."

And so Paul went his way—alone. He smoked and drank with the fellows and sat for hours in the Montmartre cafes and never knew the companionship of a woman. Then one night after his work he was walking along the street in his queer shuffling way when a woman stepped up to his side.

"Voulez vous."

"Naw, gowan away from here."

"Oh, you speak English, don't you?"

"You an 'merican woman?"

"Used to be 'fore I went on the stage and got stranded over here."

"Well, get away from here. I don't like your kind!"

"Aw, Buddy, don't say that. I ain't prejudiced like some fool women."

"You don't know who I am, do you? I'm Paul Watson and I hate American white folks, see?"

He pushed her aside and went on walking alone. He hadn't gone far when she caught up to him and said with sobs in her voice:—

"Oh, Lordy, please don't hate me 'cause I was born white and an American. I ain't got a sou to my name and all the men pass me by cause I ain't spruced up. Now you come along and won't look at me cause I'm white."

Paul strode along with her clinging to his arm. He tried to shake her off several times but there was no use. She clung all the more desperately to him. He looked down at her frail body shaken with sobs, and something caught at his heart. Before he knew what he was doing he had said:—

"Naw, I ain't that mean. I'll get you some grub. Quit your cryin'. Don't like seein' women folks cry."

It was the talk of Montmartre. Paul Watson takes a woman to Gavarnni's every night for dinner. He comes to the Flea Pit less frequently, thus giving the other musicians plenty of opportunity to discuss him.

"How times do change. Paul, the woman-hater, has a Jane now."

"You ain't said nothing, fella. That ain't all. She's white and an 'merican, too."

"That's the way with these spades. They beat up all the white men they can lay their hands on but as soon as a gang of golden hair with blue eyes rubs up close to them they forget all they ever said about hatin' white folks."

"Guess he thinks that skirt's gone on him. Dumb fool!"

"Don' be no chineeman. That old gag don' fit for Paul. He cain't understand it no more'n we can. Says he jess can't help himself, everytime she looks up into his eyes and asks him does he love her. They sure are happy together. Paul's goin' to marry her, too. At first she kept saying that she didn't want to get married cause she wasn't the marrying kind and all that talk. Paul jus' laid down the law to her and told him he never would live with no woman without being married to her. Then she began to tell him all about her past life. He told her he didn't care nothing about what she used to be jus' so long as they loved each other now. Guess they'll make it."

"Yeah, Paul told me the same tale last night. He's sure gone on her all right."

"They're gettin' tied up next Sunday. So glad it's not me. Don't trust these American dames. Me for the Frenchies."

"She ain't so worse for looks, Bud. Now that he's been furnishing the green for the rags."

"Yeah, but I don't see no reason for the wedding bells. She was right—she ain't the marrying kind."

. . . and so Montmartre talked. In every cafe where the Negro musicians congregated Paul Watson was the topic for conversation. He had suddenly fallen from his place as bronze God to almost less than the dust.

The morning sun made queer patterns on Paul's sleeping face. He grimaced several times in his slumber, then finally half-opened his eyes. After a succession of dream-laden blinks he gave a great yawn, and rubbing his eyes, looked at the open window through which the sun shone brightly. His first conscious thought was that this was the bride's day and that bright sunshine prophesied happiness for the bride throughout her married life. His first impulse was to settle back into the covers and think drowsily about Mary and the queer twists life brings about, as is the wont of most bridegrooms on their last morning of bachelorhood. He put this impulse aside in favor of dressing quickly and rushing downstairs to telephone to Mary to say "happy wedding day" to her.

One huge foot slipped into a worn bedroom slipper and then the other dragged painfully out of the warm bed were the courageous beginnings of his bridal toilette. With a look of triumph he put on his new grey suit that he had ordered from an English tailor. He carefully pulled a taffeta tie into place beneath his chin, noting as he looked at his face in the mirror that the scar he had received in the army was very ugly—funny, marrying an ugly man like him.

French telephones are such human faults. After trying for about fifteen minutes to get Central 32.01 he decided that he might as well walk around to Mary's hotel to give his greeting as to stand there in the lobby of his own, wasting his time. He debated this in his mind a great deal. They were to be married at four o'clock. It was eleven now and it did seem a shame not to let her have a minute or two by herself. As he went walking down the street towards her hotel he laughed to think of how one always cogitates over doing something and finally does the thing he wanted to in the beginning anyway.

Mud on his nice gray suit that the English tailor had made for him. Damn—gray suit—what did he have a gray suit on for, anyway. Folks with black faces shouldn't wear gray suits. Gawd, but it was funny that time when he beat up that cracker at the Periquet. Fool couldn't shut his mouth he was so surprised. Crackers—damn 'em—he was one nigger that wasn't 'fraid of 'em. Wouldn't he have a hell of a time if he went back to America where black was black. Wasn't white nowhere, black wasn't. What was that thought he was trying to get ahold of—bumping around in his head—something he started to think about but couldn't remember it somehow.

The shrill whistle that is typical of the French subway pierced its way into his thoughts. Subway —why was he in the subway—he didn't want to go any place. He heard doors slamming and saw the blue uniforms of the conductors swinging on to the cars as the trains began to pull out of the station. With one or two strides he reached the last coach as it began to move up the platform. A bit out of breath he stood inside the train and looking down at what he had in his hand he saw that it was a tiny pink ticket. A first class ticket in a second class coach. The idea set him to laughing. Everyone in the car turned and eyed him, but that did not bother him. Wonder what stop he'd get off—funny how these French said descend when they meant get off—funny he couldn't pick up French—been here so long. First class ticket in a second class coach! —that was one on him. Wedding day today, and that damn letter from Mary. How'd she say it now, "just couldn't go through with it," white women just don't marry colored men, and she was a street woman, too. Why couldn't she have told him flat that she was just getting back on her feet at his expense. Funny that first class ticket he bought, wish he could see Mary—him a-going there to wish her "happy wedding day," too. Wonder what that French woman was looking at him so hard for? Guess it was the mud.

GWENDOLYN BENNETT.

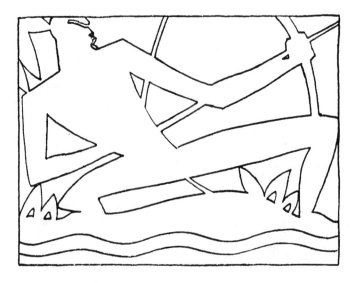

Three Drawings

Aaron Douglas

Smoke, Lilies and Jade

He wanted to do something . . . to write or draw . . . or something . . . but it was so comfortable just to lay there on the bed . . . . . . his shoes off . . . and think . . . think of everything . . . short disconnected thoughts—to wonder . . . to remember . . . to think and smoke . . . why wasn't he worried that he had no money . . . he *had* had five cents . . . but he had been hungry . . . he *was* hungry and still . . . all he wanted to do was . . . lay there comfortably smoking . . . think . . . wishing he were writing . . . or drawing . . . or something . . . something about the things he felt and thought . . . but what did he think . . . he remembered how his mother had awakened him one night . . . ages ago . . . six years ago . . . Alex . . . he had always wondered at the strangeness of it . . . she had seemed so . . . so . . . so just the same . . . Alex . . . I think your father is dead . . . and it hadn't seemed so strange . . . yet . . . one's mother didn't say that . . . didn't wake one at midnight every night to say . . . feel him . . . put your hand on his head . . . then whisper with a catch in her voice . . . I'm afraid . . . sh don't wake Lam . . . yet it hadn't seemed as it should have seemed . . . even when he had felt his father's cool wet forehead . . . it hadn't been tragic . . . the light had been turned very low . . . and flickered . . . yet it hadn't been tragic . . . or weird . . . not at all as one should feel when one's father died . . . even his reply of . . . yes he is dead . . . had been commonplace . . . hadn't been dramatic . . . there had been no tears . . . no sobs . . . not even a sorrow . . . and yet he must have realized that one's father couldn't smile . . . or sing any more . . . after he had died . . . every one remembered his father's voice . . . it had been a lush voice . . . a promise . . . then that dressing together . . . his mother and himself . . . in the bathroom . . . why was the bathroom always the warmest room in the winter . . . as they had put on their clothes . . . his mother had been telling him what he must do . . . and cried softly . . . and that had made him cry too but you mustn't cry Alex . . . remember you have to be a little man now . . . and that was all . . . didn't other wives and sons cry more for their dead than that . . . anyway people never cried for beautiful sunsets . . . or music . . . and those were the things that hurt . . . the things to sympathize with . . . then out into the snow and dark of the morning . . . first to the undertaker's . . . no first to Uncle Frank's . . .why did Aunt Lula have to act like that . . . to ask again and again . . . but when did he die . . .

when did he die . . . I just can't believe it . . . poor Minerva . . . then out into the snow and dark again . . . how had his mother expected him to know where to find the night bell at the undertaker's . . . he was the most sensible of them all tho . . . all he had said was . . . what . . . Harry Francis . . . too bad . . . tell mamma I'll be there first thing in the morning . . . then down the deserted streets again . . . to grandmother's . . . it was growing light now . . . it must be terrible to die in daylight . . . grandpa had been sweeping the snow off the yard . . . he had been glad of that because . . . well he could tell him better than grandma . . . grandpa . . . father's dead . . . and he hadn't acted strange either . . . books lied . . . he had just looked at Alex a moment then continued sweeping . . . all he said was . . . what time did he die . . . she'll want to know . . . then passing thru the lonesome street toward home . . . Mrs. Mamie Grant was closing a window and spied him . . . hallow Alex . . . an' how's your father this mornin' . . . dead . . . get out . . . tch tch tch an' I was just around there with a cup a' custard yesterday . . . Alex puffed contentedly on his cigarette . . . he was hungry and comfortable . . . and he had an ivory holder inlaid with red jade and green . . . funny how the smoke seemed to climb up that ray of sunlight . . . went up the slant just like imagination . . . was imagination blue . . . or was it because he had spent his last five cents and couldn't worry . . . anyway it was nice to lay there and wonder . . . and remember . . . why was he so different from other people . . . the only things he remebered of his father's funeral were the crowded church and the ride in the hack . . . so many people there in the church . . . and ladies with tears in their eyes . . . and on their cheeks . . . and some men too . . . why did people cry . . . vanity that was all . . . yet they weren't exactly hypocrites . . . but why . . . it had made him furious . . . all these people crying . . . it wasn't *their* father . . . and he wasn't crying . . . couldn't cry for sorrow altho he had loved his father more than . . . than . . . it had made him so angry that tears had come to his eyes . . . and he had been ashamed of his mother . . . crying into a handkerchief . . . so ashamed that tears had run down his cheeks and he had frowned . . . and some one . . . a woman . . . had said . . . look at that poor little dear . . . Alex is just like his father . . . and the tears had run fast . . . because he *wasn't* like his father . . . he couldn't sing . . . he didn't want to sing . . . he didn't want to sing . . . Alex blew a cloud of smoke . . . blue smoke . . . when they had taken his father from the vault three weeks later . . . he had grown beautiful . . . his nose had become perfect and clear . . . his hair had turned jet black and glossy and silky . . . and his skin was a transparent green . . . like the sea only not so deep . . . and where it was drawn over the cheek bones a pale beautiful red appeared . . . like a blush . . . why hadn't his father looked like that always . . . but no . . . to have sung would have broken the wondrous repose of his lips and maybe that was his beauty . . . maybe it was wrong to think thoughts like these . . . but they were nice and pleasant and comfortable . . . when one was smoking a cigarette thru an ivory holder . . . inlaid with red jade and green . . . .

he wondered why he couldn't find work . . . a job . . . when he had first come to New York he had . . . and he had only been fourteen then was it because he was nineteen now that he felt so idle . . . and contented . . . or because he was an artist . . . but was he an artist . . . was one an artist until one became known . . . of course he was an artist . . . and strangely enough so were all his friends . . . he should be ashamed that he didn't work . . . but . . . was it five years in New York . . . or the fact that he was an artist . . . when his mother said she couldn't understand him . . . why did he vaguely pity her instead of being ashamed . . . he should be . . . his mother and all his relatives said so . . . his brother was three years younger than he and yet he had already been away from home a year . . . on the stage . . . making thirty-five dollars a week . . . had three suits and many clothes and was going to help mother . . . while he . . . Alex . . . was content to lay and smoke and meet friends at night . . . to argue and read Wilde . . . Freud . . . Boccacio and Schnitzler . . . to attend Gurdjieff meetings and know things . . . Why did they scoff at him for knowing such people as Carl . . . Mencken . . . Toomer . . . Hughes . . . Cullen . . . Wood . . . Cabell . . . oh the whole lot of them . . . was it because it seemed incongruous that he . . . who was so little known . . . should call by first names people they would like to know . . . were they jealous . . . no mothers aren't jealous of their sons . . . they are proud of them . . . why then . . . when these friends accepted and liked him . . . no matter how he dressed . . . why did mother ask . . . and you went looking like that . . . Langston was a fine fellow . . . he knew there was something in Alex . . . and so did Rene and Borgia . . . and Zora and Clement and Miguel . . . and . . . and . . . and all of them . . . if he went to see mother she would ask . . . how do you

feel Alex with nothing in your pockets . . . I don't see how you can be satisfied . . . Really you're a mystery to me . . . and who you take after . . . I'm sure I don't know . . . none of my brothers were lazy and shiftless . . . I can never remember the time when they weren't sending money home and your father was your age he was supporting a family . . . where you get your nerve I don't know . . . just because you've tried to write one or two little poems and stories that no one understands . . . you seem to think the world owes you a living . . . you should see by now how much is thought of them . . . you can't sell anything . . . and you won't do anything to make money . . . wake up Alex . . . I don't know what will become of you . . . .

it was hard to believe in one's self after that . . . did Wildes' parents or Shelly's or Goya's talk to them like that . . . but it was depressing to think in that vein . . . Alex stretched and yawned . . . Max had died . . . Margaret had died . . . so had Sonia . . . Cynthia . . . Juan-Jose and Harry . . . all people he had loved . . . loved one by one and together . . . and all had died . . . he never loved a person long before they died . . . in truth he was tragic . . . that was a lovely appellation . . . The Tragic Genius . . . think . . . to go thru life known as The Tragic Genius . . . romantic . . . but it was more or less true . . . Alex turned over and blew another cloud of smoke . . . was all life like that . . . smoke . . . blue smoke from an ivory holder . . . he wished he were in New Bedford . . . New Bedford was a nice place . . . snug little houses set complacently behind protecting lawns . . . half open windows showing prim interiors from behind waving cool curtains . . . inviting . . . like precise courtesans winking from behind lace fans . . . and trees . . . many trees . . . casting lacey patterns of shade on the sun dipped sidewalks . . . small stores . . . naively proud of their psuedo grandeur . . . banks . . . called institutions for saving . . . all naive . . . that was it . . . New Bedford was naive . . . after the sophistication of New York it would fan one like a refreshing breeze . . . and yet he had returned to New York . . . and sophistication . . . was he sophisticated . . . no because he was seldom bored . . . seldom bored by anything . . . and weren't the sophisticated continually suffering from ennui . . . on the contrary . . . he was amused . . . amused by the artificiality of naivety and sophistication alike . . . but may be that in itself was the essence of sophistication or . . . was it cynicism . . . or were the two identical . . . he blew a cloud of smoke . . . it was growing dark now . . . and the smoke no longer had a ladder to climb . . . but soon the moon would rise and then he would

clothe the silver moon in blue smoke garments . . .
truly smoke was like imagination . . . .

Alex sat up . . . pulled on his shoes and went out
. . . it was a beautiful night . . . and so large . . . the
dusky blue hung like a curtain in an immense arched
doorway . . . fastened with silver tacks . . . to wan-
der in the night was wonderful . . . myriads of in-
quisitive lights . . . curiously prying into the dark
. . . and fading unsatisfied . . . he passed a woman
. . . she was not beautiful . . . and he was sad because
she did not weep that she would never be beautiful
. . . was it Wilde who had said . . . a cigarette is
the most perfect pleasure because it leaves one unsatisfied . . . the breeze gave to him a perfume stolen
from some wandering lady of the evening . . . it
pleased him . . . why was it that men wouldn't use
perfumes . . . they should . . . each and every one of
them liked perfumes . . . the man who denied that
was a liar . . . or a coward . . . but if ever he were
to voice that thought . . . express it . . . he would be
misunderstood . . . a fine feeling that . . . to be misunderstood . . . it made him feel tragic and great
. . . but may be it would be nicer to be understood
. . . but no . . . no great artist is . . . then again
neither were fools . . . they were strangely akin
these two . . . Alex thought of a sketch he would
make . . . a personality sketch of Fania . . . straight
classic features tinted proud purple . . . sensuous
fine lips . . . gilded for truth . . . eyes . . . half
opened and lids colored mysterious green . . . hair
black and straight . . . drawn sternly mocking back
from the false puritanical forehead . . . maybe he
would made Edith too . . . skin a blue . . . infinite
like night . . . and eyes . . . slant and grey . . . very
complacent like a cat's . . . Mona Lisa lips . . . red
and seductive as . . . as pomegranate juice . . . in
truth it was fine to be young and hungry and an
artist . . . to blow blue smoke from an ivory holder
. . . .

here was the cafeteria . . . it was almost as tho it
had journeyed to meet him . . . the night was so
blue . . . how does blue feel . . . or red or gold or
any other color . . . if colors could be heard he could
paint most wondrous tunes . . . symphonious . . .
think . . . the dulcet clear tone of a blue like night
. . . of a red like pomegranate juice . . . like Edith's
lips . . . of the fairy tones to be heard in a sunset
. . . like rubies shaken in a crystal cup . . . of the
symphony of Fania . . . and silver . . . and gold . . .
he had heard the sound of gold . . . but they weren't
the sounds he wanted to catch . . . no . . . they must
be liquid . . . not so staccato but flowing variations
of the same caliber . . . there was no one in the
cafe as yet . . . he sat and waited . . . that was a

clever idea he had had about color music . . . but
after all he was a monstrous clever fellow . . .
Jurgen had said that . . . funny how characters in
books said the things one wanted to say . . . he
would like to know Jurgen . . . how does one go
about getting an introduction to a fiction character
. . . go up to the brown cover of the book and knock
gently . . . and say hello . . . then timidly . . . is
Duke Jurgen there . . . or . . . no because if entered
the book in the beginning Jurgen would only be a
pawn broker . . . and one didn't enter a book in the
center . . . but what foolishness . . . Alex lit a cigarette . . . but Cabell was a master to have written
Jurgen . . . and an artist . . . and a poet . . . Alex
blew a cloud of smoke . . . a few lines of one of
Langston's poems came to describe Jurgen . . . . .

> Somewhat like Ariel
> Somewhat like Puck
> Somewhat like a gutter boy
> Who loves to play in muck.
> Somewhat like Bacchus
> Somewhat like Pan
> And a way with women
> Like a sailor man . . . .

Langston must have known Jurgen . . . suppose
Jurgen had met Tonio Kroeger . . . what a vagrant
thought . . . Kroeger . . . Kroeger . . . Kroeger . . .
why here was Rene . . . Alex had almost gone to
sleep . . . Alex blew a cone of smoke as he took
Rene's hand . . . it was nice to have friends like Rene
. . . so comfortable . . . Rene was speaking . . .
Borgia joined them . . . and de Diego Padro . . .
their talk veered to . . . James Branch Cabell . . .
beautiful . . . marvelous . . . Rene had an enchanting
accent . . . said sank for thank and souse for south
. . . but they couldn't know Cabell's greatness . . .
Alex searched the smoke for expression . . . he . . .
he . . . well he has created a phantasy mire . . . that's
it . . . from clear rich imagery . . . life and silver
sands . . . that's nice . . . and silver sands . . .
imagine lilies growing in such a mire . . . when they
close at night their gilded underside would protect
. . . but that's not it at all . . . his thoughts just
carried and mingled like . . . like odors . . . sug-
gested but never definite . . . Rene was leaving . . .
they all were leaving . . . Alex sauntered slowly
back . . . the houses all looked sleepy . . . funny
. . . made him feel like writing poetry . . . and about
death too . . . an elevated crashed by overhead scat-
tering all his thoughts with its noise . . . making
them spread . . . in circles . . . then larger circles
. . . just like a splash in a calm pool . . . what had
he been thinking . . . of . . . a poem about death . . .

but he no longer felt that urge . . . just walk and think and wonder . . . think and remember and smoke . . . blow smoke that mixed with his thoughts and the night . . . he would like to live in a large white palace . . . to wear a long black cape . . . very full and lined with vermillion . . . to have many cushions and to lie there among them . . . talking to his friends . . . lie there in a yellow silk shirt and black velvet trousers . . . like music-review artists talking and pouring strange liquors from curiously beautiful bottles . . . bottles with long slender necks . . . he climbed the noisy stair of the odorous tenement . . . smelled of fish . . . of stale fried fish and dirty milk bottles . . . he rather liked it . . . he liked the acrid smell of horse manure too . . . strong . . . thoughts . . . yes to lie back among strangely fashioned cushions and sip eastern wines and talk . . . Alex threw himself on the bed . . . removed his shoes . . . stretched and relaxed . . . yes and have music waft softly into the darkened and incensed room . . . he blew a cloud of smoke . . . oh the joy of being an artist and of blowing blue smoke thru an ivory holder inlaid with red jade and green . . .

⌣

the street was so long and narrow . . . so long and narrow . . . and blue . . . in the distance it reached the stars . . . and if he walked long enough . . . far enough . . . he could reach the stars too . . . the narrow blue was so empty . . . quiet . . . Alex walked music . . . it was nice to walk in the blue after a party . . . Zora had shone again . . . her stories . . . she always shone . . . and Monty was glad . . . every one was glad when Zora shone . . . he was glad he had gone to Monty's party . . . Monty had a nice place in the village . . . nice lights . . . and friends and wine . . . mother would be scandalized that he could think of going to a party . . . without a copper to his name . . . but then mother had never been to Monty's . . . and mother had never seen the street seem long and narrow and blue . . . Alex walked music . . . the click of his heels kept time with a tune in his mind . . . he glanced into a lighted cafe window . . . inside were people sipping coffee . . . men . . . why did they sit there in the loud light . . . didn't they know that outside the street . . . the narrow blue street met the stars . . . that if they walked long enough . . . far enough . . . Alex walked and the click of his heels sounded . . . and had an echo . . . sound being tossed back and forth . . . back and forth . . . some one was approaching . . . and their echoes mingled . . . and gave the sound of castenets . . . Alex liked the sound of the approaching man's footsteps . . . he walked music also . . . he knew the beauty of the

narrow blue . . . Alex knew that by the way their echoes mingled . . . he wished he would speak . . . but strangers don't speak at four o'clock in the morning . . . at least if they did he couldn't imagine what would be said . . . maybe . . . pardon me but are you walking toward the stars . . . yes, sir, and if you walk long enough . . . then may I walk with you I want to reach the stars too . . . perdone me senor tiene vd. fosforo . . . Alex was glad he had been addressed in Spanish . . . to have been asked for a match in English . . . or to have been addressed in English at all . . . would have been blasphemy just then . . . Alex handed him a match . . . he glanced at his companion apprehensively in the match glow . . . he was afraid that his appearance would shatter the blue thoughts . . . and stars . . . ah . . . his face was a perfect compliment to his voice . . . and the echo of their steps mingled . . . they walked in silence . . . the castanets of their heels clicking accompaniment . . . the stranger inhaled deeply and with a nod of content and a smile . . . blew a cloud of smoke . . . Alex felt like singing . . . the stranger knew the magic of blue smoke also . . . they continued in silence . . . the castanets of their heels clicking rythmically . . . Alex turned in his doorway . . . up the stairs and the stranger waited for him to light the room . . . no need for words . . . they had always known each other . . . . as they undressed by the blue dawn . . . Alex knew he had never seen a more perfect being . . . his body was all symmetry and music . . . and Alex called him Beauty . . . long they lay . . . blowing smoke and exchanging thoughts . . . and Alex swallowed with difficulty . . . he felt a glow of tremor . . . and they talked and . . . slept . . .

Alex wondered more and more why he liked Adrian so . . . he liked many people . . . Wallie . . . Zora . . . Clement . . . Gloria . . . Langston . . . John . . . Gwenny . . . oh many people . . . and they were friends . . . but Beauty . . . it was different . . . once Alex had admired Beauty's strength . . . and Beauty's eyes had grown soft and he had said . . . I like you more than any one Dulce . . . Adrian always called him Dulce . . . and Alex had become confused . . . was it that he was so susceptible to beauty that Alex liked Adrian so much . . . but no . . . he knew other people who were beautiful . . . Fania and Gloria . . . Monty and Bunny . . . but he was never confused before them . . . while Beauty . . . Beauty could make him believe in Buddha . . . or imps . . . and no one else could do that . . . that is no one but Melva . . . but then he was in love with Melva . . . and that explained that . . . he would like Beauty to know

Melva . . . they were both so perfect . . . such compliments . . . yes he would like Beauty to know Melva because he loved them both . . . there . . . he had thought it . . . actually dared to think it . . . but Beauty must never know . . . Beauty couldn't understand . . . indeed Alex couldn't understand . . . and it pained him . . . almost physically . . . and tired his mind . . . Beauty . . . Beauty was in the air . . . the smoke . . . Beauty . . . Melva . . . Beauty . . . Melva . . . Alex slept . . . and dreamed . . . . .

he was in a field . . . a field of blue smoke and black poppes and red calla lilies . . . he was searching . . . on his hands and knees . . . searching . . . among black poppies and red calla lilies . . . he was searching pushed aside poppy stems . . . and saw two strong white legs . . . dancer's legs . . . the contours pleased him . . . his eyes wandered . . . on past the muscular hocks to the firm white thighs . . . the rounded buttocks . . . then the lithe narrow waist . . . strong torso and broad deep chest . . . the heavy shoulders . . . the graceful muscled neck . . . squared chin and quizzical lips . . . grecian nose with its temperamental nostrils . . . the brown eyes looking at him . . . like . . . Monty looked at Zora . . . his hair curly and black and all tousled . . . and it was Beauty . . . and Beauty smiled and looked at him and smiled . . . said . . . I'll wait Alex . . . and Alex became confused and continued his search . . . on his hands and knees . . . pushing aside poppy stems and lily stems . . . a poppy . . . a black poppy . . . a lilly . . . a red lilly . . . and when he looked back he could no longer see Beauty . . . Alex continued his search . . . thru poppies . . . lilies . . . poppies and red calla lilies . . . and suddenly he saw . . . two small feet olive-ivory . . . two well turned legs curving gracefully from slender ankles . . . and the contours soothed him . . . he followed them . . . past the narrow rounded hips to the tiny waist . . . the fragile firm breasts . . . the graceful slender throat . . . the soft rounded chin . . . slightly parting lips and straight little nose with its slightly flaring nostrils . . . the black eyes with lights in them . . . looking at him . . . the forehead and straight cut black hair . . . and it was Melva . . . and she looked at him and smiled and said . . . I'll wait Alex . . . and Alex became confused and kissed her . . . became confused and continued his search . . . on his hands and knees . . . pushed aside a poppy stem . . . a black-poppy stem . . . pushed aside a lily stem . . . a red-lily stem . . . a poppy . . . a poppy . . . a lily . . . and suddenly he stood erect . . . exhultant . . . and in his hand he held . . . an ivory holder . . . inlaid with red jade . . . and green . . . .

and Alex awoke . . . Beauty's hair tickled his nose

. . . Beauty was smiling in his sleep . . . half his face stained flush color by the sun . . . the other half in shadow . . . blue shadow . . . his eye lashes casting cobwebby blue shadows on his cheek . . . his lips were so beautiful . . . quizzical . . . Alex wondered why he always thought of that passage from Wilde's Salome . . . when he looked at Beauty's lips . . . I would kiss your lips . . . he *would* like to kiss Beauty's lips . . . Alex flushed warm . . . with shame . . . or was it shame . . . he reached across Beauty for a cigarette . . . Beauty's cheek felt cool to his arm . . . his hair felt soft . . . Alex lay smoking . . . such a dream . . . red calla lilies . . . red calla lilies . . . and . . . what could it all mean . . . did dreams have meanings . . . Fania said . . . and black poppies . . . thousands . . . millions . . . Beauty stirred . . . Alex put out his cigarette . . . closed his eyes . . . he mustn't see Beauty yet . . . speak to him . . . his lips were too hot . . . dry . . . the palms of his hands too cool and moist . . . thru his half closed eyes he could see Beauty . . . propped . . . cheek in hand . . . on one elbow . . . looking at him . . . lips smiling quizzically . . . he wished Beauty wouldn't look so hard . . . Alex was finding it difficult to breathe . . . breathe normally . . . why *must* Beauty look so long . . . and smile *that* way . . . his face seemed nearer . . . it was . . . Alex could feel Beauty's hair on his forehead . . . breathe normally . . . breathe normally . . . could feel Beauty's breath on his nostrils and lips . . . and it was clean and faintly colored with tobacco . . . breathe normally Alex . . . Beauty's lips were nearer . . . Alex closed his eyes . . . how did one act . . . his pulse was hammering . . . from wrists to finger tip . . . wrist to finger tip . . . Beauty's lips touched his . . . his temples throbbed . . . throbbed . . . his pulse hammered from wrist to finger tip . . . Beauty's breath came short now . . . softly staccato . . . breathe normally Alex . . . you are asleep . . . Beauty's lips touched his . . . breathe normally . . . and pressed . . . pressed hard . . . cool . . . his body trembled . . . breathe normally Alex . . . Beauty's lips pressed cool . . . cool and hard . . . how much pressure does it take to waken one . . . Alex sighed . . . moved softly . . . how does one act . . . Beauty's hair barely touched him now . . . his breath was faint on . . . Alex's nostrils . . . and lips . . . Alex stretched and opened his eyes . . . Beauty was looking at him . . . propped on one elbow . . . cheek in his palm . . . Beauty spoke . . . scratch my head please Dulce . . . Alex was breathing normally now . . . propped against the bed head . . . Beauty's head in his lap . . . Beauty spoke . . . I wonder why I like to look at some things Dulce . . . things like smoke and cats . . . and you . . . Alex's pulse no longer hammered from . . . wrist to finger tip . . . wrist to finger tip . . . the rose dusk had become blue night . . . and soon . . . soon they would go out into the blue . . . .

✺

the little church was crowded . . . warm . . . the rows of benches were brown and sticky . . . Harold was there . . . and Constance and Langston and Bruce and John . . . there was Mr. Robeson . . . how are you Paul . . . a young man was singing . . . Caver . . . Caver was a very self assured young man . . . such a dream . . . poppies . . . black poppies . . . they were applauding . . . Constance and John were exchanging notes . . . the benches were sticky . . . a young lady was playing the piano . . . fair . . . and red calla lilies . . . who had ever heard of red calla lilies . . . they were applauding . . . a young man was playing the viola . . . what could it all mean . . . so many poppies . . . and Beauty looking at him like . . . like Monty looked at Zora . . . another young man was playing a violin . . . he was the first real artist to perform . . . he had a touch of soul . . . or was it only feeling . . . they were hard to differentiate on the violin . . . and Melva standing in the poppies and lilies . . . Mr. Phillips was singing . . . Mr. Phillips was billed as a basso . . . and he had kissed her . . . they were applauding . . . the first young man was singing again . . . Langston's spiritual . . . Fy-ah-fy-ah-Lawd . . . fy-ah's gonna burn ma soul . . . Beauty's hair was so black and curly . . . they were applauding . . . encore . . . Fy-ah Lawd had been a success . . . Langston bowed . . . Langston had written the words . . . Hall bowed . . . Hall had written the music . . . the young man was singing it again . . . Beauty's lips had pressed hard . . . cool . . . cool . . . fy-ah Lawd . . . his breath had trembled . . . fy-ah's gonna burn ma soul . . . they were all leaving . . . first to the roof dance . . . fy-ah Lawd . . . there was Catherine . . . she was beautiful tonight . . . she always was at night . . . Beauty's lips . . . fy-ah Lawd . . . hello Dot . . . why don't you take a boat that sails . . . when are you leaving again . . . and there's Estelle . . . every one was there . . . fy-ah Lawd . . . Beauty's body had pressed close . . . close . . . fy-ah's gonna burn my soul . . . let's leave . . . have to meet some people at the New World . . . then to Augusta's party . . . Harold . . . John . . . Bruce . . . Connie . . . Langston . . . ready . . . down one hundred thirty-fifth street . . . fy-ah . . . meet these people and leave . . . fy-ah Lawd . . . now to Augusta's party . . . fy-ahs gonna burn ma soul . . . they were at Augusta's . . . Alex half lay . . . half sat on the floor . . . sipping a cocktail . . . such a dream . . . red calla lilies . . .

Alex left . . . down the narrow streets . . . fy-ah . . . up the long noisy stairs . . . fy-ahs gonna bu'n ma soul . . . his head felt swollen . . . expanding . . . contracting . . . expanding . . . contracting . . . he had never been like this before . . . expanding . . . contracting . . . it was that . . . fy-ah . . . fy-ah Lawd . . . and the cocktails . . . and Beauty . . . he felt two cool strong hands on his shoulders . . . it was Beauty . . . lie down Dulce . . . Alex lay down . . . Beauty . . . Alex stopped . . . no no . . . don't say it . . . Beauty mustn't know . . . Beauty couldn't understand . . . are you going to lie down too Beauty . . . the light went out expanding . . . contracting . . . he felt the bed sink as Beauty lay beside him . . . his lips were dry . . . hot . . . the palms of his hands so moist and cool . . . Alex partly closed his eyes . . . from beneath his lashes he could see Beauty's face over his . . . nearer . . . nearer . . . Beauty's hair touched his forehead now . . . he could feel his breath on his nostrils and lips . . . Beauty's breath came short . . . breathe normally Beauty . . . breathe normally . . . Beauty's lips touched his . . . pressed hard . . . cool . . . opened slightly . . . Alex opened his eyes . . . into Beauty's . . . parted his lips . . . Dulce . . . Beauty's breath was hot and short . . . Alex ran his hand through Beauty's hair . . . Beauty's lips pressed hard against his teeth . . . Alex trembled . . . could feel Beauty's body . . . close against his . . . hot . . . tense . . . white . . . and soft . . . soft . . . soft . . . .

✺

they were at Forno's . . . every one came to Forno's once maybe only once . . . but they came . . . see that big fat woman Beauty . . . Alex pointed to an overly stout and bejeweled lady making her way thru the maize of chairs . . . that's Maria Guerrero . . . Beauty looked to see a lady guiding almost the whole opera company to an immense table . . . really Dulce . . . for one who appreciates beauty you do use the most abominable English . . . Alex lit a cigarette . . . and that florid man with white hair . . . that's Carl . . . Beauty smiled . . . The Blind bow boy . . . he asked . . . Alex wondered . . . everything seemed to . . . so just the same . . . here they were laughing and joking about people . . . there's Rene . . . Rene this is my friend Adrian . . . after that night . . . and he felt so unembarrassed . . . Rene and Adrian were talking . . . there was Lucricia Bori . . . she was bowing at their table . . . oh her cousin was with them . . . and Peggy Joyce . . . every one came to Forno's . . . Alex looked toward the door . . . there was Melva . . . Alex beckoned . . . Melva this is Adrian . . . Beauty held her hand . . . they talked . . . smoked . . . Alex loved Melva . . . in

Forno's . . . every one came there sooner or later . . . maybe once . . . but . . . .

up . . . up . . . slow . . . jerk up . . . up . . . not fast . . . not glorious . . . but slow . . . up . . . up into the sun . . . slow . . . sure like fate . . . poise on the brim . . . the brim of life . . . two shining rails straight down . . . Melva's head was on his shoulder . . . his arm was around her . . . poise . . . the down . . . gasping . . . straight down . . . straight like sin . . . down . . . the curving shiny rail rushed up to meet them . . . hit the bottom then . . . shoot up . . . fast . . . glorious . . . up into the sun . . . Melva gasped . . . Alex's arm tightened . . . all goes up . . . then down . . . straight like hell . . . all breath squeezed out of them . . . Melva's head on his shoulder . . . up . . . up . . . Alex kissed her . . . down . . . they stepped out of the car . . . walking music . . . now over to the Ferris Wheel . . . out and up . . . Melva's hand was soft in his . . . out and up . . . over mortals . . . mortals drinking nectar . . . five cents a glass . . . her cheek was soft on his . . . up . . . up . . . till the world seemed small . . . tiny . . . the ocean seemed tiny and blue . . . up . . . up and out . . . over the sun . . . the tiny red sun . . . Alex kissed her . . . up . . . up . . . their tongues touched . . . up . . . seventh heaven . . . the sea had swallowed the sun . . . up and out . . . her breath was perfumed . . . Alex kissed her . . . drift down . . . soft . . . soft . . . the sun had left the sky flushed . . . drift down . . . soft down . . . back to earth . . . visit the mortals sipping nectar at five cents a glass . . . Melva's lips brushed his . . . then out among the mortals . . and the sun had left a flush on Melva's cheeks . . . they walked hand in hand . . . and the moon came out . . . they walked in silence on the silver strip . . . and the sea sang for them . . . they walked toward the moon . . . we'll hang our hats on the crook of the moon Melva . . . softly on the silver strip . . . his hands molded her features and her cheeks were soft and warm to his touch . . . where is Adrian . . . Alex . . . Melva trod silver . . . Alex trod sand . . . Alex trod sand . . . the sea *sang* for her . . . Beauty . . . her hand felt cold in his . . . Beauty . . . the sea *dinned* . . . Beauty . . . he led the way to the train . . . and the train dinned . . . Beauty . . . dinned . . . dinned . . . her cheek *had* been soft . . . Beauty . . . Beauty . . . her breath *had* been perfumed . . . Beauty . . . Beauty . . . the sands *had* been silver . . . Beauty . . . Beauty . . . they left the train . . . Melva walked music . . . Melva said . . . don't make me blush again . . . and kissed him . . . Alex stood on the steps after she left him and the night was black . . . down long streets to . . . Alex lit a cigarette . . . and his heels clicked . . . Beauty . . . Melva . . . Beauty . . . Melva . . . and the smoke made the night blue . . .

Melva had said . . . don't make me blush again . . . and kissed him . . . and the street had been blue . . . one *can* love two at the same time . . . Melva had kissed him . . . one *can* . . . and the street had been blue . . . one *can* . . . and the room was clouded with blue smoke . . . drifting vapors of smoke and thoughts . . . Beauty's hair was so black . . . and soft . . . blue smoke from an ivory holder . . . was that why he loved Beauty . . . one *can* . . . or because his body was beautiful . . . and white and warm . . . or because his eyes . . . one *can* love . . . .

RICHARD BRUCE.

. . . To Be Continued . . .

Sweat

It was eleven o'clock of a Spring night in Florida. It was Sunday. Any other night, Delia Jones would have been in bed for two hours by this time. But she was a washwoman, and Monday morning meant a great deal to her. So she collected the soiled clothes on Saturday when she returned the clean things. Sunday night after church, she sorted them and put the white things to soak. It saved her almost a half day's start. A great hamper in the bedroom held the clothes that she brought home. It was so much neater than a number of bundles lying around.

She squatted in the kitchen floor beside the great pile of clothes, sorting them into small heaps according to color, and humming a song in a mournful key, but wondering through it all where Sykes, her husband, had gone with her horse and buckboard.

Just then something long, round, limp and black fell upon her shoulders and slithered to the floor beside her. A great terror took hold of her. It softened her knees and dried her mouth so that it was a full minute before she could cry out or move. Then she saw that it was the big bull whip her husband liked to carry when he drove.

She lifted her eyes to the door and saw him standing there bent over with laughter at her fright. She screamed at him.

"Sykes, what you throw dat whip on me like dat? You know it would skeer me—looks just like a snake, an' you knows how skeered Ah is of snakes."

"Course Ah knowed it! That's how come Ah done it." He slapped his leg with his hand and almost rolled on the ground in his mirth. "If you such a big fool dat you got to have a fit over a earth worm or a string, Ah don't keer how bad Ah skeer you."

"You aint got no business doing it. Gawd knows it's a sin. Some day Ah'm gointuh drop dead from some of yo' foolishness. 'Nother thing, where you been wid mah rig? Ah feeds dat pony. He aint fuh you to be drivin' wid no bull whip."

"You sho is one aggravatin' nigger woman!" he declared and stepped into the room. She resumed her work and did not answer him at once. "Ah done tole you time and again to keep them white folks' clothes outa dis house."

He picked up the whip and glared down at her. Delia went on with her work. She went out into the yard and returned with a galvanized tub and sit it on the washbench. She saw that Sykes had kicked all of the clothes together again, and now stood in her way truculently, his whole manner hoping, *praying,* for an argument. But she walked calmly around him and commenced to re-sort the things.

"Next time, Ah'm gointer kick 'em outdoors," he threatened as he struck a match along the leg of his corduroy breeches.

Delia never looked up from her work, and her thin, stooped shoulders sagged further.

"Ah aint for no fuss t'night Sykes. Ah just come from taking sacrament at the church house."

He snorted scornfully. "Yeah, you just come from de church house on a Sunday night, but heah you is gone to work on them clothes. You ain't nothing but a hypocrite. One of them amen-corner Christians—sing, whoop, and shout, then come home and wash white folks clothes on the Sabbath."

He stepped roughly upon the whitest pile of things, kicking them helter-skelter as he crossed the room. His wife gave a little scream of dismay, and quickly gathered them together again.

"Sykes, you quit grindin' dirt into these clothes! How can Ah git through by Sat'day if Ah don't start on Sunday?"

"Ah don't keer if you never git through. Anyhow, Ah done promised Gawd and a couple of other men, Ah aint gointer have it in mah house. Don't gimme no lip neither, else Ah'll throw 'em out and put mah fist up side yo' head to boot."

Delia's habitual meekness seemed to slip from her shoulders like a blown scarf. She was on her feet; her poor little body, her bare knuckly hands bravely defying the strapping hulk before her.

"Looka heah, Sykes, you done gone too fur. Ah been married to you fur fifteen years, and Ah been takin' in washin' fur fifteen years. Sweat, sweat, sweat! Work and sweat, cry and sweat, pray and sweat!"

"What's that got to do with me?" he asked brutally.

"What's it got to do with you, Sykes? Mah tub of suds is filled yo' belly with vittles more times than yo' hands is filled it. Mah sweat is done paid for this house and Ah reckon Ah kin keep on sweatin' in it."

She seized the iron skillet from the stove and struck a defensive pose, which act surprised him greatly, coming from her. It cowed him and he did not strike her as he usually did.

"Naw you won't," she panted, "that ole snaggle-toothed black woman you runnin' with aint comin' heah to pile up on *mah* sweat and blood. You aint paid for nothin' on this place, and Ah'm gointer stay right heah till Ah'm toted out foot foremost."

"Well, you better quit gittin' me riled up, else they'll be totin' you out sooner than you expect. Ah'm so tired of you Ah don't know whut to do. Gawd! how Ah hates skinny wimmen!"

A little awed by this new Delia, he sidled out of the door and slammed the back gate after him. He did not say where he had gone, but she knew too well. She knew very well that he would not return until nearly daybreak also. Her work over, she went on to bed but not to sleep at once. Things had come to a pretty pass!

She lay awake, gazing upon the debris that cluttered their matrimonial trail. Not an image left standing along the way. Anything like flowers had long ago been drowned in the salty stream that had been pressed from her heart. Her tears, her sweat, her blood. She had brought love to the union and he had brought a longing after the flesh. Two months after the wedding, he had given her the first brutal beating. She had the memory of his numerous trips to Orlando with all of his wages when he had returned to her penniless, even before the first year had passed. She was young and soft then, but now she thought of her knotty, muscled limbs, her harsh knuckly hands, and drew herself up into an unhappy little ball in the middle of the big feather bed. Too late now to hope for love, even if it were not Bertha it would be someone else. This case differed from the others only in that she was bolder than the others. Too late for everything except her little home. She had built it for her old days, and planted one by one the trees and flowers there. It was lovely to her, lovely.

Somehow, before sleep came, she found herself saying aloud: "Oh well, whatever goes over the Devil's back, is got to come under his belly. Sometime or ruther, Sykes, like everybody else, is gointer reap his sowing." After that she was able to build a spiritual earthworks against her husband. His shells could no longer reach her. *Amen*. She went to sleep and slept until he announced his presence in bed by kicking her feet and rudely snatching the cover away.

"Gimme some kivah heah, an' git yo' damn foots over on yo' own side! Ah oughter mash you in yo' mouf fuh drawing dat skillet on me."

Delia went clear to the rail without answering him. A triumphant indifference to all that he was or did.

The week was as full of work for Delia as all other weeks, and Saturday found her behind her little pony, collecting and delivering clothes.

It was a hot, hot day near the end of July. The village men on Joe Clarke's porch even chewed cane listlessly. They did not hurl the cane-knots as usual. They let them dribble over the edge of the porch. Even conversation had collapsed under the heat.

"Heah come Delia Jones," Jim Merchant said, as the shaggy pony came 'round the bend of the road toward them. The rusty buckboard was heaped with baskets of crisp, clean laundry.

"Yep," Joe Lindsay agreed. "Hot or col', rain or shine, jes ez reg'lar ez de weeks roll roun' Delia carries 'em an' fetches 'em on Sat'day."

"She better if she wanter eat," said Moss. "Syke Jones aint wuth de shot an' powder hit would tek tuh kill 'em. Not to *huh* he aint."

"He sho' aint," Walter Thomas chimed in. "It's too bad, too, cause she wuz a right pritty lil trick when he got huh. Ah'd uh mah'ied huh mah-seff if he hadnter beat me to it."

Delia nodded briefly at the men as she drove past.

"Too much knockin' will ruin *any* 'oman. He done beat huh 'nough tuh kill three women, let 'lone change they looks," said Elijah Mosely. "How Syke kin stommuck dat big black greasy Mogul he's layin' roun' wid, gits me. Ah swear dat eight-rock couldn't kiss a sardine can Ah done thowed out de back do' 'way las' yeah."

"Aw, she's fat, thass how come. He's allus been crazy 'bout fat women," put in Merchant. "He'd a' been tied up wid one long time ago if he could a' found one tuh have him. Did Ah tell yuh 'bout him come sidlin' roun' *mah* wife—bringin' her a basket uh pee-cans outa his yard fuh a present? Yessir, mah wife! She tol' him tuh take 'em right straight back home, cause Delia works so hard ovah dat washtub she reckon everything on de place taste lak sweat an' soapsuds. Ah jus' wisht Ah'd a' caught 'im 'roun' dere! Ah'd a' made his hips ketch on fiah down dat shell road."

"Ah know he done it, too. Ah sees 'im grinnin' at every 'oman dat passes," Walter Thomas said. "But even so, he useter eat some mighty big hunks uh humble pie tuh git dat lil' 'oman he got. She wuz ez pritty ez a speckled pup! Dat wuz fifteen yeahs ago. He useter be so skeered uh losin' huh, she could make him do some parts of a husband's duty. Dey never wuz de same in de mind."

"There oughter be a law about him," said Lindsay. He aint fit tuh carry guts tuh a bear."

Clarke spoke for the first time. "Taint no law on earth dat kin make a man be decent if it aint in 'im. There's plenty men dat takes a wife lak dey do a joint uh sugar-cane. It's round, juicy an' sweet when dey gits it. But dey squeeze an' grind, squeeze an' grind an' wring tell dey wring every drop uh pleasure dat's in 'em out. When dey's satisfied dat dey is wrung dry, dey treats 'em jes lak dey do a cane-chew. Dey thows 'em away. Dey knows whut dey is doin' while dey is at it, an' hates theirselves fuh it but they keeps on hangin' after huh tell she's empty. Den dey hates huh fuh bein' a cane-chew an' in de way."

"We oughter take Syke an' dat stray 'oman uh his'n down in Lake Howell swamp an' lay on de rawhide till they cain't say 'Lawd a' mussy.' He allus wuz uh ovahbearin' niggah, but since dat white 'oman from up north done teached 'im how to run a automobile, he done got to biggety to live—an' we oughter kill 'im." Old Man Anderson advised.

A grunt of approval went around the porch. But the heat was melting their civic virtue and Elijah Moseley began to bait Joe Clarke.

"Come on, Joe, git a melon outa dere an' slice it up for yo' customers. We'se all sufferin' wid de heat. De bear's done got *me!*"

"Thass right, Joe, a watermelon is jes' whut Ah needs tuh cure de eppizudicks," Walter Thomas joined forces with Moseley. "Come on dere, Joe. We all is steady customers an' you aint set us up in a long time. Ah chooses dat long, bowlegged Floridy favorite."

"A god, an' be dough You all gimme twenty cents and slice away," Clarke retorted. "Ah needs a col' slice m'self. Heah, everybody chip in. Ah'll lend y'll mah meat knife."

The money was quickly subscribed and the huge melon brought forth. At that moment, Sykes and Bertha arrived. A determined silence fell on the porch and the melon was put away again.

Merchant snapped down the blade of his jack-knife and moved toward the store door.

"Come on in, Joe, an' gimme a slab uh sow belly an' uh pound uh coffee—almost fuhgot 'twas Sat'-day. Got to git on home." Most of the men left also.

Just then Delia drove past on her way home, as Sykes was ordering magnificently for Bertha. It pleased him for Delia to see.

"Git whutsoever yo' heart desires, Honey. Wait a minute, Joe. Give huh two botles uh strawberry soda-water, uh quart uh parched ground-peas, an' a block uh chewin' gum."

With all this they left the store, with Sykes reminding Bertha that this was his town and she could have it if she wanted it.

The men returned soon after they left, and held their watermelon feast.

"Where did Syke Jones git dat 'oman from nohow?" Lindsay asked.

"Ovah Apopka. Guess dey musta been cleanin' out de town when she lef'. She don't look lak a thing but a hunk uh liver wid hair on it."

"Well, she sho' kin squall," Dave Carter contributed. "When she gits ready tuh laff, she jes' opens huh mouf an' latches it back tuh de las' notch. No ole grandpa alligator down in Lake Bell ain't got nothin' on huh."

❧

Bertha had been in town three months now. Sykes was still paying her room rent at Della Lewis'—the only house in town that would have taken her in. Sykes took her frequently to Winter Park to "stomps." He still assured her that he was the swellest man in the state.

"Sho' you kin have dat lil' ole house soon's Ah kin git dat 'oman outa dere. Everything b'longs tuh me an' you sho' kin have it. Ah sho' 'bominates uh skinny 'oman. Lawdy, you sho' is got one portly shape on you! You kin git *anything* you wants. Dis is *mah* town an' you sho' kin have it."

Delia's work-worn knees crawled over the earth in Gethsemane and up the rocks of Calvary many, many times during these months. She avoided the villagers and meeting places in her efforts to be blind and deaf. But Bertha nullified this to a degree, by coming to Delia's house to call Sykes out to her at the gate.

Delia and Sykes fought all the time now with no peaceful interludes. They slept and ate in silence. Two or three times Delia had attempted a timid friendliness, but she was repulsed each time. It was plain that the breaches must remain agape.

❧

The sun had burned July to August. The heat streamed down like a million hot arrows, smiting all things living upon the earth. Grass withered, leaves browned, snakes went blind in shedding and men and dogs went mad. Dog days!

Delia came home one day and found Sykes there before her. She wondered, but started to go on into the house without speaking, even though he was standing in the kitchen door and she must either stoop under his arm or ask him to move. He made no room for her. She noticed a soap box beside the steps, but paid no particular attention to it, knowing that he must have brought it there. As she was stooping to pass under his outstretched arm, he suddenly pushed her backward, laughingly.

"Look in de box dere Delia, Ah done brung yuh somethin'!"

She nearly fell upon the box in her stumbling, and when she saw what it held, she all but fainted outright.

"Syke! Syke, mah Gawd! You take dat rattlesnake 'way from heah! You *gottuh.* Oh, Jesus, have mussy!"

"Ah aint gut tuh do nuthin' uh de kin'—fact is Ah aint got tuh do nothin' but die. Taint no use uh you puttin' on airs makin' out lak you skeered uh dat snake—he's gointer stay right heah tell he die. He wouldn't bite me cause Ah knows how tuh handle 'im. Nohow he wouldn't risk breakin' out his fangs 'gin *yo'* skinny laigs."

"Naw, now Syke, don't keep dat thing 'roun' heah tuh skeer me tuh death. You knows Ah'm even feared uh earth worms. Thass de biggest snake Ah evah did see. Kill 'im Syke, please."

"Doan ast me tuh do nothin' fuh yuh. Goin' 'roun' tryin' tuh be so damn asterperious. Naw, Ah aint gonna kill it. Ah think uh damn sight mo' uh him dan you! Dat's a nice snake an' anybody doan lak 'im kin jes' hit de grit."

The village soon heard that Sykes had the snake, and came to see and ask questions.

"How de hen-fire did you ketch dat six-foot rattler, Syke?" Thomas asked.

"He's full uh frogs so he caint hardly move, thass how Ah eased up on 'm. But Ah'm a snake charmer an' knows how tuh handle 'em. Shux, dat aint nothin'. Ah could ketch one eve'y day if Ah so wanted tuh."

"Whut he needs is a heavy hick'ry club leaned real heavy on his head. Dat's de bes 'way tuh charm a rattlesnake."

"Naw, Walt, y'll jes' don't understand dese diamon' backs lak Ah do," said Sykes in a superior tone of voice.

The village agreed with Walter, but the snake stayed on. His box remained by the kitchen door with its screen wire covering. Two or three days later it had digested its meal of frogs and literally came to life. It rattled at every movement in the kitchen or the yard. One day as Delia came down the kitchen steps she saw his chalky-white fangs curved like scimitars hung in the wire meshes. This time she did not run away with averted eyes as usual. She stood for a long time in the doorway in a red fury that grew bloodier for every second that she regarded the creature that was her torment.

That night she broached the subject as soon as Sykes sat down to the table.

"Syke, Ah wants you tuh take dat snake 'way fum heah. You done starved me an' Ah put up widcher, you done beat me an Ah took dat, but you done kilt all mah insides bringin' dat varmint heah."

Sykes poured out a saucer full of coffee and drank it deliberately before he answered her.

"A whole lot Ah keer 'bout how you feels inside uh out. Dat snake aint goin' no damn wheah till Ah gits ready fuh 'im tuh go. So fur as beatin' is concerned, yuh aint took near all dat you gointer take ef yuh stay 'roun' *me.*"

Delia pushed back her plate and got up from the table. "Ah hates you, Sykes," she said calmly. "Ah hates you tuh de same degree dat Ah useter love yuh. Ah done took an' took till mah belly is full up tuh mah neck. Dat's de reason Ah got mah letter fum de church an' moved mah membership tuh Woodbridge—so Ah don't haftuh take no sacrament wid yuh. Ah don't wantuh see yuh 'roun' me atall. Lay 'roun' wid dat 'oman all yuh wants tuh, but gwan 'way fum me an' mah house. At hates yuh lak uh suck-egg dog."

Sykes almost let the huge wad of corn bread and collard greens he was chewing fall out of his mouth in amazement. He had a hard time whipping himself up to the proper fury to try to answer Delia.

"Well, Ah'm glad you does hate me. Ah sho' tiahed uh you hangin' ontuh me. Ah don't want yuh. Look at yuh stringey ole neck! Yo' rawbony laigs an' arms is enough tuh cut uh man tuh death. You looks jes' lak de devvul's doll-baby tuh *me.* You cain't hate me no worse dan Ah hates you. Ah been hatin' *you* fuh years.

"Yo' ole black hide don't look lak nothin' tuh me, but uh passle uh wrinkled up rubber, wid yo' big ole yeahs flappin' on each side lak up paih uh buzzard wings. Don't think Ah'm gointuh be run 'way fum mah house neither. Ah'm goin' tuh de white folks bout *you,* mah young man, de very nex' time you lay yo' han's on me. Mah cup is done run ovah." Delia said this with no signs of fear and Sykes departed from the house, threatening her, but made not the slightest move to carry out any of them.

That night he did not return at all, and the next day being Sunday, Delia was glad that she did not have to quarrel before she hitched up her pony and drove the four miles to Woodbridge.

She stayed to the night service—"love feast"—which was very warm and full of spirit. In the emotional winds her domestic trials were borne far and wide so that she sang as she drove homeward,

"Jurden water, black an' col'
Chills de body, not de soul
An' Ah wantah cross Jurden in uh calm time."

She came from the barn to the kitchen door and stopped.

"Whut's de mattah, ol' satan, you aint kickin' up yo' racket?" She addressed the snake's box. Complete silence. She went on into the house with a new hope in its birth struggles. Perhaps her threat to go to the white folks had frightened Sykes! Perhaps he was sorry! Fifteen years of misery and suppression had brought Delia to the place where she would hope *anything* that looked towards a way over or through her wall of inhibitions.

She felt in the match safe behind the stove at once for a match. There was only one there.

"Dat niggah wouldn't fetch nothin' heah tuh save his rotten neck, but he kin run thew whut Ah brings quick enough. Now he done toted off nigh on tuh haff uh box uh matches. He done had dat 'oman heah in mah house, too."

Nobody but a woman could tell how she knew this even before she struck the match. But she did and it put her into a new fury.

Presently she brought in the tubs to put the white things to soak. This time she decided she need not bring the hamper out of the bedroom; she would go in there and do the sorting. She picked up the pot-bellied lamp and went in. The room was small and the hamper stood hard by the foot of the white iron bed. She could sit and reach through the bedposts—resting as she worked.

"Ah wantah cross Jurden in uh calm time." She was singing again. The mood of the "love feast" had returned. She threw back the lid of the basket almost gaily. Then, moved by both horror and terror, he spring back toward the door. *There lay the snake in the basket!* He moved sluggishly at first, but even as she turned round and round, jumped up and down in an insanity of fear, he began to stir vigorously. She saw him pouring his awful beauty from the basket upon the bed, then she seized the lamp and ran as fast as she could to the kitchen. The wind from the open door blew out the light and the darkness added to her terror. She sped to the darkness of the yard, slamming the door after her before she thought to set down the lamp. She did not feel safe even on the ground, so she climbed up in the hay barn.

There for an hour or more she lay sprawled upon the hay a gibbering wreck.

Finally she grew quiet, and after that, coherent thought. With this, stalked through her a cold, bloody rage. Hours of this. A period of introspection, a space of retrospection, then a mixture of both. Out of this an awful calm.

"Well, Ah done de bes' Ah could. If things aint right, Gawd knows taint mah fault."

She went to sleep—a twitchy sleep—and woke up to a faint gray sky. There was a loud hollow sound below. She peered out. Sykes was at the wood-pile, demolishing a wire-covered box.

He hurried to the kitchen door, but hung outside there some minutes before he entered, and stood some minutes more inside before he closed it after him.

The gray in the sky was spreading. Delia descended without fear now, and crouched beneath the low bedroom window. The drawn shade shut out the dawn, shut in the night. But the thin walls held back no sound.

"Dat ol' scratch is woke up now!" She mused at the tremendous whirr inside, which every woodsman knows, is one of the sound illusions. The rattler is a ventriloquist. His whirr sounds to the right, to the left, straight ahead, behind, close under foot—everywhere but where it is. Woe to him who guesses wrong unless he is prepared to hold up his end of the argument! Sometimes he strikes without rattling at all.

Inside, Sykes heard nothing until he knocked a pot lid off the stove while trying to reach the match safe in the dark. He had emptied his pockets at Bertha's.

The snake seemed to wake up under the stove and Sykes made a quick leap into the bedroom. In spite of the gin he had had, his head was clearing now.

"Mah Gawd!" he chattered, "ef Ah could on'y strack uh light!"

The rattling ceased for a moment as he stood paralyzed. He waited. It seemed that the snake waited also.

"Oh, fuh de light! Ah thought he'd be too sick"—Sykes was muttering to himself when the whirr began again, closer, right underfoot this time. Long before this, Sykes' ability to think had been flattened down to primitive instinct and he leaped —onto the bed.

Outside Delia heard a cry that might have come from a maddened chimpanzee, a stricken gorilla. All the terror, all the horror, all the rage that man possibly could express, without a recognizable human sound.

A tremendous stir inside there, another series of animal screams, the intermittent whirr of the reptile. The shade torn violently down from the window, letting in the red dawn, a huge brown hand seizing the window stick, great dull blows upon the wooden floor punctuating the gibberish of sound long after the rattle of the snake had abruptly subsided. All this Delia could see and hear from her place beneath the window, and it made her ill. She crept over to the four-o'clocks and stretched herself on the cool earth to recover.

She lay there. "Delia, Delia!" She could hear Sykes calling in a most despairing tone as one who expected no answer. The sun crept on up, and he called. Delia could not move—her legs were gone flabby. She never moved, he called, and the sun kept rising.

"Mah Gawd!" She heard him moan, "Mah Gawd fum Heben!" She heard him stumbling about and got up from her flower-bed. The sun was growing warm. As she approached the door she heard him call out hopefully, "Delia, is dat you Ah heah?"

She saw him on his hands and knees as soon as she reached the door. He crept an inch or two toward her—all that he was able, and she saw his horribly swollen neck and is one open eye shining with hope. A surge of pity too strong to support bore her away from that eye that must, could not, fail to see the tubs. He would see the lamp. Orlando with its doctors was too far. She could scarcely reach the Chinaberry tree, where she waited in the growing heat while inside she knew the cold river was creeping up and up to extinguish that eye which must know by now that she knew.

ZONA NEALE HURSTON.

Intelligentsia

Of all the doughty societies that have sprung up in this age of Kluxers and Beavers the one known by that unpronounceable word, "Intelligentsia," is among the most benighted. The war seems to have given it birth, the press nurtured it, which should have been warning enough, then the public accepted it, and now we all suffer.

Of course no one would admit that he is a member of the Intelligentsia. Modern civilizing influences do not develop that kind of candor. But it is just as easy to spot a member of the genus as it is to spot a Mississippian or a Chinese: the marks are all there.

According to the ultra-advanced notions of the great majority of this secret order if it were not for the Intelligentsia this crippled old world would be compelled to kick up its toes and die on the spot. Were it not for these super-men all the brilliance of the ages and the inheritance which is so vital to the maintenance of the spark of progress would vanish and pass away. In other words if the Intelligentsia were to stick their divinely appointed noses a little higher into the ethereal regions and withdraw themselves completely from the tawdry field of life that field would soon become a burial ground for the rest of humanity.

This is the rankest folly. The world owes about as much to the rank and file of this society as a Negro slave owes to Georgia. Besides a few big words added to the lexicon and one or two hifalutin' notions about the way the world should be run, the contribution of Intelligentsia to society is as negligible as gin at a Methodist picnic. This is not to discount the many notable contributions by really intelligent men and women who didn't know that such a society existed until insignificant nincompoops with their eyes set towards enhancing their own positions in society, made them honorary members.

What is intelligence anyway? If you ask a member of the Intelligentsia he will probably sneer at you and ask who wants to know. The Intelligentsia are very particular about observing the admonition against putting a herd of swine on an oyster diet, so particular in fact that they have become much more adept at discovering pigpens than they are at digging pearls. But if you ask a truly intelligent person he will tell you in a jiffy that intelligence is simply the ability to solve a new problem, nothing more, nothing less.

Now that is just what the average member of the Intelligentsia does not do. He does not solve new problems, he makes them; then he leaves it to the true intellectuals to solve them. Sift the chaff out of Intelligentsia and you will find that the residuum is about fifty-six one hundredths of one per cent. For the rest, the society is made up of non-producers and bloodsuckers who feed voraciously on the bones which the true intellectuals pass on to them to pick over.

The average member of Intelligentsia comes as near being a true intellectual as the proverbial hot water in which resides a cabbage leaf comes to being stew. His earmarks are abundant information about the most recent literature, an obsession for the latest shows, wild notions about art in general, along with a flair for disdaining Babbits, and for feigning spiritual chumminess with the true intellectuals who are accomplishing things.

He reads H. L. M. and George Jean Nathan, knows his Freud from cover to cover, and has an ability for spotting morons which is positively as uncanny as the ability of a Texas bloodhound to sniff a nigger. If he's a man he is as incapable of attending to his own affairs and doing something once in a while, as a hobo is incapable of paying a month's rent. All this goes for the feminine Intelligentsia, with this added distinction—they sneer at every homely virtue, including taking care of babies and frying eggs without breaking the yolks.

Far be it from me to sing paens to the days when men amused themselves with dominoes and the fair sex waded through enough dishwater to make a Jordan. Those days and their folk hold no illusions for me. But it is high time that a halt is called on these snobbish sycophantish highbrow hero-worshippers who, having got a smattering of wisdom from one of the fifty-seven hundred purveyors of this rare article in America, deign to damn with their sneers and jibes any activity, institution, or mortal it strikes their fancy to treat in such a manner.

These are the folk who talk Bolshevism in their parlors and wouldn't go to Russia if it were placed, like milk for cats, in saucers on their doorsteps. They slur Beethoven or Tennyson and extol Stravinsky and Whitman when they are hardly able to grasp such simple minded folk as Leybach or Longfellow, or even Eddie Guest himself.

They mull over best sellers and can call authors' names by the scores. Literature for them is measured by its mystic qualities or its pornographical settings; music by its aberrations from generally accepted forms; art by its illusiveness.

Anything that is plain or clear or clean comes under the suspicion of these folk if not actually beneath their contempt. They who themselves do almost nothing by way of contributing to the nation's artistic development set themselves up as the struggling workman's severest critics. Ofttimes they are actually proud of their non-accomplishment: it shows their artistic temperament, they boast. Good God deliver us from their art!

One can admire truly intellectual types like Sinclair Lewis, Dreiser, H.L.M., and Shaw, men who are in every respect creative critics and thinkers. What one cannot swallow is this carrion prostrated at the altar of Liberalism when as a matter of fact their lying hearts are as faint as they are insipid. Their pelts are as mangy as Main Streeters' and their sentiments as hypocritical as those of the most pious Kluxer in the Bible Belt. They are by far more to be despised than the "morons" whom they single out with such avidity; for the latter do at least make an attempt to earn their salt, and to express themselves honestly, while the Intelligentsia steal all they can get away with and never do anything unless it be in the attitude of a dethroned prince who suddenly has to go to work.

These folk have no more right to become associated with true artistic spirits than Knights of Columbus have to drink the Grand Kleagle's health. They simply give art and artists a black eye with their snobbery and stupidity; and their false interpretations and hypocritical evaluations do more to heighten suspicion against the real artist on the part of the ordinary citizen than perhaps any other single factor in the clash of art and provincialism.

Certainly there is more excuse for innocent idiocy and moronesia than there is for the sophisticated bigotry of these fair folk who, in the secret recesses of their inner consciousness, lay claim to membership in the Intelligentsia.

ARTHUR HUFF FAUSET.

Fire Burns

A Department of Comment

Some time ago, while reviewing Carl Van Vechten's lava laned Nigger Heaven I made the prophecy that Harlem Negroes, once their aversion to the "nigger" in the title was forgotten, would erect a statue on the corner of 135th Street and Seventh Avenue, and dedicate it to this ultra-sophisticated Iowa New Yorker.

So far my prophecy has failed to pan out, and superficially it seems as if it never will, for instead of being enshrined for his pseudo-sophisticated, semi-serious, semi-ludicrous effusion about Harlem, Mr. Van Vechten is about to be lynched, at least in effigy.

Yet I am loathe to retract or to temper my first prophecy. Human nature is too perverse and prophecies do not necessarily have to be fulfilled within a generation. Rather, they can either be fulfilled or else belied with startling two-facedness throughout a series of generations, which, of course, creates the possibility that the fulfillments may outnumber the beliements and thus gain credence for the prophecy with posterity. Witness the Bible.

However, in defending my prophecy I do not wish to endow Mr. Van Vechten's novel (?) with immortality, but there is no real reason why Nigger Heaven should not eventually be as stupidly acclaimed as it is now being stupidly damned by the majority of Harlem's dark inhabitants. Thus I defiantly reiterate that a few years hence Mr. Van Vechten will be spoken of as a kindly gent rather than as a moral leper exploiting people who had believed him to be a sincere friend.

I for one, and strange as it may sound, there are others, who believe that Carl Van Vechten was rendered sincere during his explorations and observations of Negro life in Harlem, even if he remained characteristically superficial. Superficiality does not necessarily denote a lack of sincerity, and even superficiality may occasionally delve into deep pots of raw life. What matter if they be flesh pots?

In writing Nigger Heaven the author wavered between sentimentality and sophistication. That the sentimentality won out is his funeral. That the sophistication stung certain Negroes to the quick is their funeral.

The odds are about even. Harlem cabarets have received another public boost and are wearing out cash register keys, and entertainers' throats and orchestra instruments. The so-called intelligentsia of Harlem has exposed its inherent stupidity. And Nigger Heaven is a best seller.

Group criticism of current writings, morals, life, politics, or religion is always ridiculous, but what could be more ridiculous than the wholesale condemnation of a book which only one-tenth of the condemnators have or will read. And even if the book was as vile, as degrading, and as defamatory to the character of the Harlem Negro as the Harlem Negro now declares, his criticisms would not be considered valid by an intelligent person as long as the critic had had no reading contact with the book.

The objectors to Nigger Heaven claim that the author came to Harlem, ingratiated himself with Harlem folk, and then with a supercilious grin and a salacious smirk, lolled at his desk downtown and dashed off a pornographic document about uptown in which all of the Negro characters are pictured as being debased, lecherous creatures not at all characteristic or true to type, and that, moreover, the author provokes the impression that all of Harlem's inhabitants are cabaret hounds and thirsty neurotics. He did not tell, say his critics, of our well bred, well behaved church-going majorities, nor of our night schools filled with eager elders, nor of our brilliant college youth being trained in the approved contemporary manner, nor of our quiet, home loving thousands who hardly know what the word cabaret connotes. He told only of lurid night life and of uninhibited sybarites. Therefore, since he has done these things and neglected to do these others the white people who read the book will believe that all Harlem Negroes are like the Byrons, the Lascas, the Pettijohns, the Rubys, the Creepers, the Bonifaces, and the other lewd hussies and whoremongers in the book.

It is obvious that these excited folk do not realize that any white person who would believe such poppy-cock probably believes it anyway, without any additional aid from Mr. Van Vechten, and should such a person read a tale anent our non-cabareting, church-going Negroes, presented in all their virtue and glory and with their human traits, their human hypocrisy and their human perversities glossed over, written, say, by Jessie Fauset, said person would laugh derisively and allege that Miss Fauset had not told the truth, the same as Harlem

Negroes are alleging that Carl Van Vechten has not told the truth. It really makes no difference to the race's welfare what such ignoramuses think, and it would seem that any author preparing to write about Negroes in Harlem or anywhere else (for I hear that DuBose Heyward has been roundly denounced by Charlestonian Negroes for his beautiful Porgy) should take whatever phases of their life that seem the most interesting to him, and develop them as he pleases. Why Negroes imagine that any writer is going to write what Negroes think he ought to write about them is too ridiculous to merit consideration. It would seem that they would shy away from being pigeon-holed so long have they been the rather lamentable victims of such a typically American practice, yet Negroes would have all Negroes appearing in contemporary literature made as ridiculous and as false to type as the older school of pseudo-humorous, sentimental white writers made their Uncle Toms, they Topsys, and their Mammies, or as the Octavius Roy Cohen school now make their more modern "cullud" folk.

One young lady, prominent in Harlem collegiate circles, spoke forth in a public forum (oh yes, they even have public forums where they spend their time anouncing that they have not read the book, and that the author is a moral leper who also commits literary sins), that there was only one character in Nigger Heaven who was true to type. This character, the unwitting damsel went on, was Mary Love. It seems as if all the younger Negro women in Harlem are prototypes of this Mary Love, and it is pure, poor, virtuous, vapid Mary, to whom they point as a typical life model.

Again there has been no realization that Mary Love is the least life-life character in the book, or that it is she who suffers most from her creator's newly acquired seriousness and sentimentality, she who suffers most of the whole ensemble because her creator discovered, in his talented trippings around Manhattan, drama at which he could not chuckle the while his cavalier pen sped cleverly on in the same old way yet did not—could not spank.

But—had all the other characters in Nigger Heaven approximated Mary's standard, the statue to Carl Van Vechten would be an actualized instead of a deferred possibility, and my prophecy would be gloriously fulfilled instead of being ignominiously belied.

WALLACE THURMAN.